Captain Deadlock

Captain Deadlock

LAURENCE HYDE

Illustrated by Charles Geer

1968

Houghton Mifflin Company Boston

Also by

LAURENCE HYDE

Under the Pirate Flag

CONTENTS

For
Tony and Chris
who have gone away
to seek their fortunes.

I

I Leave to Seek My Fortune

It was the spring of the year 18— when I undertook a voyage to Plymouth, a journey by sea from my home in Glasgow. I remember very well the smells of far-off places as I boarded the brig, the shouting bustle of the crew, and the sound of lapping waves against the ship's side. I had my box containing clothes and what few possessions I cared to save, including my late uncle's telescope, a fine instrument that saw everything except the future, and this, as matters turned out, was a grievous lack.

My uncle and guardian, John Carruthers, had only recently passed away, to my great sorrow. He was a man highly regarded in his time, honest in his business dealings and kindly disposed to all those less fortunate than himself. He had been well acquainted with trade, having amassed a fortune buying and selling goods in all parts of the world, especially in North America, the Carolinas and in those islands of the Pacific Ocean where natives dive for pearls. In the last years of his life, however, a series of reverses in his trading ventures had brought about his downfall and he died penniless, a broken-hearted man.

It was my ambition to become a surgeon on a navy ship and to this end I was studying medicine and chemistry, but on the death of my uncle my studies ceased. One friend I had, a certain Captain William Mullins, a lifelong and devoted friend of my late uncle. Knowing a little of my situation, he sent for me by letter, bidding me call on him at the Jollyboat Inn, Plymouth, hinting that a place might be found for me as a midshipman in our navy. This prospect cheered me and I hastened to pack my box, relieved not only at the possibility of finding adventure and a positive start in life but also at leaving Glasgow where my uncle had lived and died, a place that held only sad memories for me now. In short, I was glad of any excuse for a sea change, and lost no time in finding a coasting brig to take me, with all speed, to Plymouth.

Here then began my journey, a modest enough voyage you might think; instead it was only the first stage in a most perilous series of events. But I was mercifully spared knowledge of the future and thought only of my prospects, my expectations and those golden hopes that all youth carries in its heart.

At the dockside I found the brig *Caledonia*, Captain Campbell, bound for Bristol and perhaps — if fortune should so decide — Plymouth. After much haggling I bought passage in her, though the Captain promised nothing beyond Bristol.

"Ye ken there's a war on," he said. "It's chancy, what with one thing and another. Unless I get suitable cargo in Bristol I'm off back to Glasgow, so take it or leave it. It's a mixed cargo I have now an' I'm willing to damn Napoleon as far as

Bristol. If I get a good cargo in Bristol, I'll damn him as far as Plymouth, for an extra two guineas."

So the bargain was sealed. I paid in advance for Bristol, deciding to cross one bridge at a time. With my money thus safely in his pocket, he became more amiable, and shouldering the box, he personally conducted me to my cabin — a mere cupboard of a place hardly big enough to swing a cat in.

"It's a mite small but the best I can do," he said, bending his head low against the beams and setting my box on the narrow bunk. He dropped his voice almost to a whisper.

"The fact is, Mr. Carruthers, another passenger came aboard, not an hour since. Took the mate's cabin and paid twice the amount and a bit over. Wants to be let alone and meals in his cabin. Mr. Blunt his name is, from Berwick, so he says, though his speech is verra queer for the Tweed. Other than that I'd be happy to give ye the mate's cabin, but ye see how it is. The mate's in with me."

I assured him of my satisfaction with the cabin, all things considered. With that he left me and went about his duties, for the *Caledonia* was due to leave within the hour. As for Mr. Blunt, I gave him not a thought; the presence of another passenger meant nothing to me.

We sailed with the tide, I watching all matters pertaining to our departure with the greatest interest. I also observed the Captain, judging him a strict, honest and fair man who knew his business. What family he had I never knew, but certain it was that his ship was his first love and entire fortune. As for enemies, he had only two that I knew about:

3

the wind and the sea itself. On the sea he spat, and he shook his fist at the wind. He fought the weather as if wind and sea were living enemies and of the voices raised in anger the gale was often the softer of the two.

From the outset the *Caledonia* was plagued by bad weather and the vessel pitched horribly in steep green seas. Her rigging moaned and whined, her Captain cursed and bellowed. With a fine disregard for nature, he crowded on the canvas. I took a grim delight in a critical examination of the mast as the press of sail managed to bend it, quite perceptibly, in the gale. Idiotically, I even put my ear against the great round timber and was amazed to hear a ghostly creaking sound, frightful enough to send a chill of alarm down my spine. Catching sight of the Captain from the tail of my eye, I quickly desisted from this odd form of entertainment. He glowered at me, making some remark about the laziness of people in general and the laziness of his own crew in particular. He said also that he was cruelly shorthanded, owing to the war. Immediately I offered my services, saying that I stood ready to obey orders as a common seaman, but he only grumbled that I was a landsman, would likely only get in the way or be washed overboard. Thus challenged I informed him that far from being a landsman I came originally from Nova Scotia where I had served on the fishing schooners and likely knew as much about work in the foretop as anyone. He looked at me gloomily and shook his head.

"There's not much of a foretop to a schooner," he said. "Besides, ye've paid yer passage. If I let ye work as crew, then ye'll be wanting yer money back — and I canna afford it."

This was so far from my mind that I only gave him a look and without another word darted up the ratlines. I was in the maintop helping with the sails before he could say nay. Glancing down I saw him looking up at me but he made no protest.

From then on I simply did what I could and helped where I appeared to be needed. But Captain Campbell was careful never to give me any direct orders, and I could tell that he still thought about the passage money.

Of the mysterious Mr. Blunt I saw little. He moved about only in the late evening when he moved at all, taking a turn around the upper deck, I suppose for exercise, and never speaking. I met him only once as I descended the quarter-deck companion, coming face to face quite unexpectedly at the foot of the stair. Light from a candle-lantern, dim and yellow, cast his face in deep shadow so that I saw, as it were, only half of him: one eye singularly malevolent in expression; one side of a nose, high and sharp, lightly marked by the pox, and half a mouth, horribly disfigured by a scar that ran from lip to cheekbone. He looked at me, it seemed, with suspicion and hatred.

We stood thus staring at each other for a brief moment, I very startled at his somber appearance and he evidently put out of countenance at our sudden meeting. Then, excusing myself and giving him a polite "good evening" (which he did not answer) I made my way past him to my cabin. I wondered a little at this singular man but beyond the merest spec-

5

ulation of a moment and a brief awareness of a strange uneasy feeling that his presence had given to me, I quickly forgot him. Moreover, early the following morning all thought of him was driven from my mind and I was not to think of Mr. Blunt again for some time to come.

About six o'clock, after breakfast (which I took with the mate, Mr. Coker) I ascended to the upper deck. Mr. Coker had told me that the carpenter had need of assistance, if I would be kind enough, and I remember going in search of him. Glancing out to sea, I noted the gray misery of the weather, the scudding clouds, the heaving restless water that stretched to the copper light of the horizon. I noted also a frigate running level with us on our starboard quarter, not above a league away.

She came out of the mist of a rain squall like a ghost, fifteen gun ports I counted, and all sail crowded on. The ports were closed but I was under no illusions on that account. I glanced around for Captain Campbell and discovered him near the poop companionway looking at the frigate through his telescope. I had the boldness to ask what he made of the vessel and whether or not she was English.

"She dinna care aboot flags," he grunted. "She's na flying one."

There was no doubt left in my mind as to her intentions and I told him so.

"Na, na," he said. "Not so hasty, laddie, never be too eager with a bad name. There's a war on an' she's perhaps a mite suspicious of us too; we're not flying much of a rag ourselves."

6

This was certainly true enough, the gale having torn our flag to shreds. Campbell ordered a new flag hoisted but the strange vessel made no like reply. Thus for me the matter was doubly settled and I was sure she was a pirate.

Captain Campbell continued to observe her through his glass, muttering to himself all the while. He was neither so foolish nor so trusting as to entirely disregard my judgment when I said flatly she was a pirate, but the fact that I, a common passenger and a boy, had been so bold as to suggest such a thing only made him favor the opposite. As she drew steadily closer he said,

"I'll make a guess she's a cautious merchant wanting a word with us. Na doot she'll be wanting her position or to pass letters." He snapped his glass shut. "Mind ye," he continued, "I'll not blame ye for yer suspicions, laddie, but ye'll observe she has na guns run oot."

At that precise moment the frigate fired a deck carronade. The ball came screaming over the rail, smashed into a water butt, bounced off the mast, and rolled into the scuppers where it finally came to rest steaming angrily, between the Captain and myself. His face was a study in surprise.

"She certainly wants a word with you, sir," I remarked, gazing at the iron ball. "There's not much doubt about it."

He glared at me, his eyes popping with rage. Then he leaped up the stair, yelling to the helmsman.

"Hold yer course!" he cried. "I'll not give way to a pirate. I'll ram before I do!"

In a sweat of alarm I watched the frigate draw closer and

closer. I thought we and the frigate would come together with such a terrible smash that both of us would go to the bottom like stones.

"I'll speak with her — in a language she'll na doot understand!" raved Campbell. "I'll not give way to any pirate. I never have, and blast me, I never will. Steady, Mr. Coker; hold to yer course!"

Poor Mr. Coker! I never saw a more unhappy man steer a ship; there he stood hunched over the wheel, his face white as a sheet.

"Captain Campbell, we'll lose the brig," he cried. "I doubt yer wisdom, sir, if I may say so."

"Then give me the wheel," snapped Campbell. "You may get the whaleboat out, Mr. Coker, if ye please, and have the men ready to abandon ship." As he took over, he gave me a sharp, frowning glance.

"Ye'd best follow the mate, Mr. Carruthers," he said sternly.

"With all due respect, sir," said I, "nothing will be gained if we all go down. If we sheer off we can yet make a fight of it."

"I'll not sheer off!" he yelled, his two great hands firmly on the wheel. "Say yer prayers, laddie!"

"With all due respect, sir," said I, "I'm neither fit nor ready to leave this world on such short notice."

"We all must go sometime," he replied. "It's up to yonder pirate. Na doot ye can swim?"

"Oh yes," I said, looking around me, I thought, for the last time. "I can swim well enough. But where to, sir?

9

There's nothing on our starboard except America; on the port side there's only Devon, and a long way it is too, for swimming!"

"Aye, it's a hard choice," he said, "and if ye stand aboot arguing the matter long enough ye'll have na choice at all. Help Mr. Coker wi' the whaleboat is my advice."

The frantic crew had little need of my help since I could see the boat hung from the falls, barely a yard or two from the heaving water.

"Perhaps you have a mind to get the logbook and sextant, sir," said I desperately. "If so, I'm quite ready to take the wheel."

"The sextant might come in handy at that," he said. He gave me a bleak look. "Verra well; keep on course, aim the ship as directed, Mr. Carruthers, or I'll flay ye alive."

With that he ran for his cabin. I took the wheel, my hands trembling. The perspiration started from my forehead and I gripped the spokes until my knuckles ached. If I had a notion of altering course, of tricking the Captain for his own good (and mine too, for that matter), any such notion was quickly dashed. Staring hopelessly at the oncoming frigate I saw there was neither sea room left, nor time. Our bowsprit now pointed directly at her stern quarter, a scant hundred yards away.

She fired a broadside at us, a futile gesture since most of the effect was wasted on the narrow target of our bow. The action smashed our figurehead (this a likeness of the goddess Aphrodite, carved, I thought, in a lively manner), also a shot tore through our lower foresail; otherwise only small damage was done.

Campbell returned quickly, thrusting sextant, log and a bag of money into my hands.

"Off wi' ye to the boat!" he cried. "I'll join ye later — if God sees fit." His expression was painful to a degree as he handed me the money; the rest of what he had to say came out with a great effort.

"If I go down with the brig," he said in a choked voice, "share the money with the crew."

I barely heard him speak. Paralyzed, unable to move, I stood there, gaping at the huge frigate, now so close that I made out the forms and faces of the pirates looking down at us. One man in particular I noted, evidently her captain, a great tall, red-bearded rogue, standing at the wheel. He snatched a pistol from his belt and fired, I thought, at Captain Campbell, though the ball sang by my ear uncomfortably close.

We missed her stern by the length of a farm gate. Somehow they managed to bring their vessel over and if they had saved their broadside till this moment, they would surely have done mortal damage to us.

Campbell shouted and raved, the big veins in his neck standing out from the pressure of his temper.

"Fire away, ye scum!" he thundered. "I've fifty barrels of gunpowder under hatches — enough to blast ye to the moon. Mr. Coker, get out the grappling irons. We'll lock onto yonder pirate and blow him sky high!"

Whether the pirates heard this awful threat I shall never know, but the news about the gunpowder came as a shock to me. I comforted myself with thinking Campbell a great liar; he had told me in Glasgow that we carried only mixed cargo.

Clutching the rail I stared after the frigate, seeing her name, *The Good Friends*, picked out in black and gold. The irony of it, I thought; they certainly stretch the meaning of friendship. As for Campbell, he shook his fist at her stern boards.

"Jacobites!" he screamed. "Stuarts!" He spun the wheel. "Bring her aboot!" he yelled to his terrified crew. "Bring her over! Smartly now!"

Leaping to their stations the men worked like demons. Never did I meet a man with a worse temper than Campbell — that is, when he was provoked. His language was blasphemous and awful. I heard him say among other things that he would smash the frigate, that it was hard enough to make an honest living without interference from pirates.

"If it's na the weather, it's the war," he raved. "If it's na the war, it's pirates — or the freight rates. I'll have na more of it!"

He glared at me.

"Mr. Carruthers, why d'ye stand there like a dummy? Away wi' ye to the boat!"

"Do you intend to ram her, Captain Campbell?" I asked, without any hope of reprieve.

"On the next tack!" he snapped. "With God's help!"

2

A Fateful Choice

Even as he spoke, a patter of rain fell upon the deck, followed a moment later by hailstones. The squall was soon about us like a curtain. Captain Campbell stared grimly after the frigate as she fell away rapidly into the mist, to vanish altogether as if she had never been.

The Captain said never a word more about running the frigate down, though I had a notion he was, in a sense, sharply disappointed. He only mopped his streaming face with a great kerchief and handed the wheel over to Mr. Coker.

"I'll trouble ye for the moneybag, Mr. Carruthers," was all he said, and when I had given him the log and sextant as well as the money he only glared at me. Then he entered his private cabin and slammed the door.

By this time, being wet through and cold, I made my way toward the galley where I might warm myself a little and even scrounge a hot mug of soup from the cook. It was then I saw Mr. Blunt perched on the lower ratlines of the mizzenmast, looking earnestly through a telescope in the direction of the vanished pirate. He was so absorbed in this occupation that he failed to notice me, nor did I go out of my way to greet him but instead went quietly about my business.

In a little while, having been treated generously by the cook, I returned, but saw nothing more of Mr. Blunt. I was destined not to catch another glimpse of him for the balance of the voyage. But once again I found his presence disturbing, the sight of him cast a curious shadow on my thoughts, and the most unreasonable speculations and suspicions flashed across my mind.

Frowning and thinking deeply on all this I was startled to hear the piercing voice of Captain Campbell hailing me from the quarterdeck.

"Avast there, Mr. Carruthers. Step forward, if ye please," he bellowed. "I'd like a brief word wi' ye, if I may."

Well, I thought, as I ascended the stair, if the captain of a vessel must needs be restrained — forcibly restrained — by a passenger, will the passenger be liable to a charge of mutiny — and perhaps hanged? Thus, bracing myself against his temper, I presently stood before him in his cabin, and to placate him, I told him that I was ready to obey his orders, to help in any way reasonable and necessary.

"Ah noo," he said kindly, "ye've acquitted yerself well aboard this ship — for a passenger, o' course. Ye had na doots, I trust, aboot the wisdom of my action against yonder pirate?"

"Oh, none at all, sir," said I, exercising, I thought, great tact and discretion. "You did the only thing possible under the circumstances."

"I'm rare glad ye think so," he said, with satisfaction. "On

14

the other hand, I must apologize for not seeing through his colors — or lack of 'em. Yer advice was sound, laddie. I'm the poorer for not taking it. It's na much of an explanation but the fact is I'm too trustful. I'm not the one ter think ill of a man or a ship until the matter's proved. The proving of it almost did for me." He sighed. "I canna make up for it except to order extra grog for the men."

"At least the enemy is driven off, sir," said I. "We owe our lives to you, if it comes to that." I was touched and surprised by his humble manner, so much indeed that I waxed extravagant in my praise in an effort to cheer him.

"Why, sir," I continued, "your imaginary gunpowder — if the pirate heard you — why, sir, your warning drove him away like a cat from a hot brick!"

"Imaginary!" cried Campbell, full of sudden indignation. "Imaginary! There's nothing imaginary aboot those fifty barrels under yer clogs, Mr. Carruthers! Aye, a fine noise it would make too, going off all at once. If a hot cannonball had fallen down the hatch — why, sir, there ain't anything imaginary aboot that, take my word for it."

Trembling a little I ventured to remind him that he carried a mixed cargo, or so he had led me to believe back in Glasgow port.

"Aye and so it is," he said sternly. "Verra mixed. I've got fifty barrels of powder for the navy and one hundred and twenty cases of cartridges for the army, all of it bound for Bristol — if we ever get there."

Unable to think of anything to say but very much chastened

15

in my thoughts, I found myself outside on the quarterdeck. He left me then, but as he walked away he turned around with an amused and wicked look in his eye.

"The cartridges, Mr. Carruthers, don't make as big a bang as the powder. Ye just get more bangs for yer money." Then he hurried away and I climbed to the lookout, where I contemplated how near we had come to hideous disaster.

As I looked out over the stormy sea I caught a last glimpse of the frigate, a slim ray of early sun gleaming on her topsail; then, as the rain closed in once more she was gone. But if *The Good Friends* had vanished from my sight, she remained much on my mind. When I slept that night I did so fitfully, my sleep broken by horrid dreams and nightmare fantasies. Finally, giving up the struggle, I decided to light the swinging candle-lantern and for the balance of the night managed to keep my eyes open by reading a book of sermons I had found somewhere about the ship. Dry stuff it was, to be sure, but the author spoke out very soundly against evil and spoke very well of Heaven, and this suited my mood and, in a way, my comfort, for I presently fell into a dreamless sleep, with the lantern still guttering from the beam.

Daylight was streaming down the hatch when I was awakened by a shout from the mate.

"Bristol dead ahead, Mr. Carruthers; dockside in about an hour if the wind holds."

Thus we came to Bristol. Captain Campbell rid himself of his dangerous cargo and had no difficulty picking up another — cork, whale oil, timber and such. All told we stayed almost three days; then, on the early morning tide, and during a most deceptive lull in the bad weather, we weighed anchor.

No sooner had we left the shelter of Bristol harbor and were fairly in the Channel when the weather, as if lying in wait, struck at us with renewed fury. We wallowed and rolled, pitched and fell away in a most sickening manner, our sails all furled except a rag to keep us head on to the heavy seas. On we struggled in the worst storms since leaving Glasgow. Off Barnstaple, the Captain decided to seek shelter, a notable victory for the weather, won against a man not easily daunted.

"This is na good for the brig," he shouted over the roaring and crashing of wind and water. "I have a mind to bide a wee in Barnstaple and get a few repairs from the carpenters, if ye'll be patient, Mr. Carruthers."

"It isn't a matter of patience, sir," I answered. "It's a matter of time, with all due respect. I'm due in Plymouth at the end of the month."

"Aye, so I understand. Ye'll be having important affairs to attend to. But I'd take it kindly if ye'd stay."

But I had no alternative and the upshot of it was that I told him that I must reach Plymouth by the thirtieth at the latest or my friend would be gone, and all things considered I would find a coach in Barnstaple for the balance of my journey.

"Weel, weel," he said, "if ye must, ye must, and I canna blame ye. It's been a rough voyage one way and another."

He looked at me very slyly as if he took me for a soft fellow who might object to a little rough weather and the occasional pirate.

"I'm no stranger to gales or pirates, Captain Campbell," I said stiffly. "I'd stay with the ship ordinarily."

"Na, na, don't take it ill," he said. "I'm only teasing ye to stay. Ye've been rare helpful — for a passenger — I'd take 'ee on as crew anytime, and so would Mr. Coker."

This was a vast compliment coming from him and I thanked him for it.

"It would be a rare pleasure if ye'd accept a wee gift," he continued, reaching into the side pocket of his coat. "A mere trifle, but ye'll na doot find it useful."

He then placed in my hand a curious knife, a folding knife hinged to a bone handle. He told me it came originally from Holland and was called a penknife. At one end was a blade, at the other a pointed steel pick for extracting stones from the hoofs of horses.

"It's a bonny tool," he said. "I've had it by me for many years."

Somehow I stammered out my thanks touched beyond measure by his surprising, unexpected generosity.

"Na na," he protested, " 'tis nothing at all. Na doot ye'll find it useful. Dinna lose it for it's rare valuable. I'll have yer box set down on the pier, soon as we dock. Ye'll na doot want to be off and away."

He shook hands with me then, wishing me good luck, enjoining me earnestly to say my prayers and avoid excess in all things. It was only later that I remembered the fare from

18

Bristol to Barnstaple. This part of the passage I had quite forgotten to pay him for. I also forgot my only fellow passenger, Mr. Blunt, little knowing — or caring — that he left the *Caledonia* like a shadow, without so much as a farewell to anyone.

Thus I took leave of the *Caledonia* and Captain Campbell. Shouldering my box, I set off over the wet cobblestones of the dockside, a steady drizzle of rain putting a damper on my spirits. Indeed, no sooner had I left the shelter of the vessel than I regretted my decision and looked back with longing at her tall masts, her spiderweb of rigging and the fine lines of her hull.

I heard a sound of distant hammering; no doubt the carpenters were already at work. As I walked away, this cheerful noise grew fainter and fainter, until, passing into a narrow street, I heard only a dreary gurgling in the gutters, the monotonous dripping of water from the eaves.

3

The Runaway Coach

An old man with a barrow directed me to a coffeehouse where, he said, a coach would arrive within the hour. He was so obviously poor that I gave him a shilling to trundle my small box and lead me to the place. Thus I found myself presently in a warm inn parlor where the landlord set good food and drink before me. By the time the coach arrived I was restored to a more cheerful frame of mind. Such a warm interval of peace and plenty! Alas, I was not to know another like it for a long time to come.

Purchasing a seat in the Ilfracombe mail, I took my place, rejoicing in the fact that I was now fairly started on the final leg of my journey to Plymouth. True, a coach is no substitute for a ship, I thought, but since I had only a small choice in the matter I settled down, resigned to make the best of it. My companions were ordinary folk, judging by appearances: a fat lady who took up enough space for two; a young husband with his pretty wife; also an older man with a small boy. The boy sucked his thumb and when I smiled, he shrank back, gazing at me with wide, fearful eyes.

We clattered out of the innyard accompanied by a great

deal of shouting and horn-blowing. Looking out of the window I noticed the rain had ceased. Few words were spoken among the passengers. The small boy fretted for a drink of water; he was told to hush and wait until the next stop. For my part I watched the passing countryside, finding it increasingly lonely and drear as the miles went by.

We had traveled halfway to the next stage when the coach was suddenly brought to a halt. Mindful of highwaymen, I leaned my head out and saw a man in a three-cornered hat talking to the coachman. The man was none other than Mr. Blunt.

He gave the coachman a box, this being placed under the coachman's seat, also a sum of money for the fare. Then he opened the door on my side and climbed in, squeezing next to the fat lady on the opposite seat, next to the window. The coach started up once more.

Mr. Blunt looked across at me and, meeting my eye, gave a start of recognition. He neither smiled nor bowed (as one might expect under the circumstances) but instead gazed at me with a look of hatred. As for me, I was so bewildered by this sudden unexpected meeting, my head in such a daze, I could only stare with my mouth open. Of course, the man had every right to take the coach if he so pleased. There was nothing strange, nothing extraordinary in Mr. Blunt's hailing the same coach that I traveled in. That I neither liked his looks nor cared for his manners was surely (as I told myself) no special cause for alarm. And yet, despite logic, all my previous feelings of disquiet regarding him came uppermost.

In a way his bad manners eased the situation: uncivil and

21

untalkative he was, therefore I was free to ignore him, to look out of the window or to read a book. Nonetheless a natural curiosity presently got the better of me; I found myself observing him in a covert way, from the corner of my eye or when his attention was directed elsewhere. He remained for a time quiet in his seat but after a while grew restless; he glared not only at me but also at the other passengers, as if they had no right to be there. Then he became agitated to the point of bobbing his head out of the window and in a deep harsh voice shouting to the coachman to go faster — or "I'll come up there and whip the horses myself."

I saw him now at close range, whereas on the *Caledonia* if I saw him at all, it was only on brief occasions, usually at a distance. But a nearer view served only to heighten my distrust and I liked him no better when I heard him talk. A closer look revealed a traveling man, for his complexion spoke of the tropics and not a little of fighting. His expression, perhaps never genial, was made even harsher by the great scar that ran down one side of his face, and this disfigurement, acquired no doubt in some deadly fight or other, set him apart from other men. In years he was perhaps closer to sixty than fifty; his clothes were faded and of a fashion long since passed away.

Grumbling and muttering, he looked presently at the little boy, who gazed back at him, thumb in mouth. The poor child shrank back upon the knee of his father, where he grizzled quietly, his face puckered up in a manner pitiful to see.

At the next staging post, in a small village, where the horses were changed, I found myself alone with Blunt. Here the other passengers (including the little boy, who stopped crying on the instant) departed to go their several ways. Since no other travelers appeared, Blunt and I were left quite alone in each other's company on the road, much to my dismay.

We rumbled forward presently. Without our previous cargo of passengers the vehicle traveled faster and easier. For a while he stared at me without speaking; I could feel his baleful gaze even though I looked from the window at the passing fields and trees.

"You're the boy from the *Caledonia*," he presently observed, blowing his nose in a large blue kerchief. He made the remark sound like an accusation.

"Quite right, sir," I replied, with more cheerfulness and politeness than I honestly felt.

"Do ye, perhaps, know who I am?" he returned, staring at me with eyes all narrow and shrewd, as if he might thrash me if I should give the wrong answer.

"Only as Mr. Blunt, a passenger on the brig, sir," said I. "Beyond that I mind my own business."

"Huffy, ain't ye!" he said, snorting. "Always talk polite to yer elders, that's the way I was brought up."

I sought hastily to change the subject of the conversation by remarking on the rough voyage and our brush with the pirate, but when I made reference to *The Good Friends*, he became quiet and withdrawn. He muttered something about bad weather and how that swab of a captain "didn't know enough to sail a milk pail, much less a brig!"

Then he leaned from the window, bobbing his head out

dangerously far to gaze earnestly and long at the road behind. He did this several times, swearing and muttering. Finally I was made so curious by all this that I plucked up my courage and I asked him what he hoped to see.

"Nothing, is what I hope," he growled, "but what I expects is another thing altogether. Trouble is what I expects, that's what." Bobbing his head back in, he blew his nose with a loud hawking sound.

"Here, boy," he said, "ye got sharp eyes. Look along the road. Tell me what ye see."

Eagerly I looked out but saw nothing except our own dust. I was keenly disappointed.

"No highwaymen at all," I said, "not the slightest sign of one."

"Highwaymen!" he snorted with fine scorn. "Them swabs!"

I asked him what else we might expect to see. He gave me no direct answer, only glared as if I were a poor half-wit.

Then, to my great alarm, he took from his side pockets two large Spanish pistols along with ball and a cannister of powder.

"What's yer name, boy?" he bellowed above the noise and rattle of the coach.

I told him.

"They call me The Bosun," he yelled, "for ye see that's what I am — a bosun, plain and simple."

Then, to my utter astonishment, he brought forth two more pistols and these he tossed to me. Well, I thought, there's nothing plain or simple about your behavior, old

fellow; you're either a great rascal or a great lunatic and the odds are you're a combination of both. I sat there goggling at him but he roughly ordered me to stand my watch and mind my business. Not wishing to provoke him, I looked out but saw only a flight of rooks and the sun low among the hills.

Never shall I forget the scene: the gloom of that swiftly moving coach; Mr. Blunt (or The Bosun as I came to think of him) with his pistols cocked and ready, sitting opposite, the shadows passing and repassing across his grim face as we rushed along. To this very day I hear the hoofbeats, the rumble of wheels, the shouting of the coachman. But most vividly of all I remember Mr. Blunt and his bleary wicked eyes gazing at me.

The end of the affair was close at hand. I looked, once more, from the window and saw three horsemen riding furiously toward us.

"Well, Mr. Blunt," I shouted, "we're being followed, sure enough."

The Bosun, with a terrible oath, leaped to the opposite window. Then he sank back into his seat and with trembling hands picked up his pistols.

"I knew it!" he cried. "It's them, right enough — and my box up with the blasted coachie! But we'll do for 'em yet. Deadlock's goin' to be shorthanded afore I'm done!"

He leaned out, shrieking to the coachman that thieves and robbers were after us, that he'd give a thousand pounds' reward if the coachman brought us through, also something about his box, though I failed to catch the sense of it because of the uproar. All this served to animate the coachman, who began whipping the horses to such a fury of effort that we slid down the hill like an avalanche.

"We'll do for 'em, I say!" cried he, bobbing his head in. "Pick up them pistols, boy; they ain't meant to scratch yer nose with!"

By now I was in a ferment of rage and anxiety — rage that this old fellow should order me about and anxiety lest his wretched affairs interrupt my journey to Plymouth — or indeed, prevent it altogether.

"Mr. Blunt, who are those men?" I asked, ignoring the pistols.

"Pirates, that's who they are," he shouted. "D'yer need an introduction? Pirates, Captain Deadlock's men — Smiley, Gimp, Sweeney — and if they catches ye they'll slit yer throat!"

"They mean nothing to me," I said. "They seem to mean a great deal to you. It's your trouble, not mine."

"You took the wrong coach, boy," he said grimly, giving me a look. Then, yelling curses, he leaned out and fired a pistol.

Suddenly, with a sharp crunch and tinkle of broken glass, one of the big lamps at the front was shattered by a bullet.

"That'll be Gimp," he observed. "Smiley and Sweeney couldn't hit a barn door with a shovel."

He turned on me in a fury.

"Afraid, ain't ye?" he raved. "A reg'lar gent and a reg'lar coward ye are. I can tell the cut of yer jib with half an eye!"

His taunts so goaded me that I snatched up the pistols. Leaning far out I fired. I remember thinking how the coachman had taken the wrong coach too, with no more say in the matter than myself. I fired the second pistol. Without another word, Mr. Blunt recharged both weapons and handed them back.

"Aim a little below the windpipe, boy," he shouted. "That way ye'll likely get 'em between the eyes."

I stuck my head out, seeing how the horsemen had now come much closer. Hopefully I fired my pistols; they exploded with a fine roar but hit nothing except the air. Then a gust of wind snatched my new sailor hat (purchased in Glasgow for the voyage) from my head. Up it flew like a bird, to vanish almost instantly amid the dust behind.

A deafening report came from above our heads as the coachman fired off a blunderbuss, but the only effect of it, so far as I could judge, was to make the horses mad with fright. Then a most shocking thing happened. I saw one of the robbers level a musket at the coachman, fire at him and hit him to such wicked effect that the poor man threw up his arms with a cry and fell to the edge of the road. I saw him briefly, lying in the dust. My heart was filled with anger and horror.

But I had no time to contemplate this tragedy. Appalled beyond measure, I realized that our coach was now driverless, a runaway pulled by mad and terrified horses. We bounced and careened from side to side in a most violent manner. Adding to my misery, I caught a grain of dust in my left eye, causing me to weep in agony.

"Damn all pirates!" I yelled. "I'll see you and your rum-soaked, thieving friends dancing at the end of a rope if I

can manage it! Damn you all, Mr. Blunt, and the devil take
you!"

"Don't swear," said The Bosun sternly. "A boy like you
should know better."

Filled with rage, I looked from the window, glaring with
bloodshot eyes at the enemy. There they were, three ugly
murderers. Having by this time reloaded, I leaned dangerously far out and fired both pistols at once. The noise was
like the roar of a cannon.

"Give 'em a broadside!" cried The Bosun, bringing his pistols to bear. "Give it to 'em — a whiff of lead, ye swabs.
Fire!"

Our aim had some effect, though whether it was Blunt's
or mine I never knew. One horseman, the one called Gimp,
had trouble keeping up and his horse bucked and reared.
This daunted the others and since they had no opportunity
to recharge without stopping they fell behind.

We had now come to a wide curve in the road and for the
moment our pursuers were hidden from view.

"Mr. Blunt," I cried, "I'm taking the driver's place. If the
horses are controlled we can make it to the next stage. I'll
need the cover of your pistols."

"Boy, ye'll never do it," he said grimly. "Jump and save
yerself, it's yer only chance."

"You're a coward and a rogue, Mr. Blunt," I said.

"That's as may be," he replied. "But I ain't a fool. Leave
the coach, I say, afore it's too late. Jump for yer life!"

I tried the handle on my side and to my dismay found it
stuck. I saw The Bosun open his door. He started climbing

for the driver's seat. I heard him scream, "They'll not get the box!" Then he seemed to lose his footing and for a moment teetered half in, half out, of the coach. I tried to pull him back and reached out my hand.

"Jump!" he cried, and vanished.

Suddenly the coach gave a most violent, sickening lurch, as if a wheel had come off. I felt myself falling in space and before I lost consciousness I remember worrying about my fine new hat. In my mind's eye I had a brief vision of it, sailing high in the air and I remember how irritated I was at the loss of it.

And then, with a flash of pain and stars, blackness overwhelmed me and I knew no more.

4

I Am Captured by Pirates

WHEN I HAD regained something of my senses, I found myself lying on the ground with the ugly face of the pirate Gimp staring down at me.

"Get up," he said roughly. "Where's The Bosun; where's his box?" I felt his hands going through my pockets as he spoke and heard him curse once or twice at the slim pickings. Well, I thought, you've put yourself to a lot of trouble for very little. All my worldly wealth consisted of one golden guinea and a penny or two. The notion that he would take even this small capital angered me to such a degree that I staggered to my feet and, giving him a push, walked toward the coach. *Walk* is hardly the word, for I staggered like a drunken man.

"Now look 'ere, Sonny," said Gimp, poking at me with his musket, "don't come it high and mighty with me. Where's Blunt and where's the box, I say?"

I ignored him (which, of course, only angered him the more) and bathed my aching head in a little brook that bubbled up nearby. This was a great relief to me and I think the coldness of the water saved my life.

While I was thus recovering my senses and easing the pain of my wounds, I could see, from the corner of my eye, the battered coach, now propped up by a log, and the pirates busily affixing one of the rear wheels.

"You're lucky to escape from that," muttered Gimp, standing behind me. "You'll need a bit more luck to escape Smiley, though. Come on, no more washin'. Up on your pins, and look sharp!"

As before, I took not the slightest notice, treating him as something less worthy of attention than a stone. Perhaps I had lost most of my wits in the accident for I acted in a most foolhardy way toward a rough, unscrupulous wretch who could easily have shot me in the back. But I braved it out in my own high-handed, reckless fashion and drank my fill there, kneeling at the brook.

Presently I felt recovered enough to argue with him. I arose to my feet, wiped my face with a corner of a sleeve and asked him what he and his companions meant by waylaying honest folk and doing murder, reminding him that it was the King's coach — that is to say, a mail coach — and if they should be caught, no mercy would be shown them and they would hang.

"Well now, Sonny, ye'd better tell this to old Smiley over there," said Gimp with a sneer. "I don't think he knows all them fearful consequences ye speak of. King's coach, was it? Well I never! Crown an' all on the door, just think of it! And you firin' from the King's own coach, bold as brass, alongside The Bosun!"

He continued to jeer and sneer, then prodded me with his

musket. This so maddened me that I went for him. My fist
found its mark. Over he fell with me on top, the musket going off with a terrible noise. Luckily the barrel pointed sky-
ward enough to fire wide, but another inch or so would have
done for me. In a moment I was pulled from Gimp by the
rough hands of Smiley and Sweeney. Despite my struggles,
my hands were tied. Thus all my brave words and bold actions came to naught.

"You little swine!" hissed Smiley. "Reg'lar tartar, ye are.
We'll knock it outa ye before we're done. Now then, where's
The Bosun? You was with him, firin' at us. Why, I'll
wring yer neck an' slit yer throat, so I will."

I told Smiley that I knew nothing about The Bosun and cared less.

"Ye'll care all right, afore we're done!" he raved. "Shootin' at honest seamen! We'll teach ye better manners, so we will, an' old Blunt too, when we catch 'im!"

He turned to Gimp and, with an oath, asked if anything was found on me.

"Nothin'," said Gimp sulkily. "Not a sign of it."

"I found the box with the lid busted open," growled Smiley. "Nothin' in it 'cept rubbish — old clothes and that. I've searched the rotten coach from stem to stern."

"Then he had the stuff on him and he's run off with it," said Sweeney.

"Run off with what?" said I, very mystified.

"Mind yer business!" shouted Smiley. "We ain't talkin' to you."

"Well, that's a relief," said I, in such a provoking way that it was a fair wonder that Smiley held himself in check. As it was, he stuck his face close up, his eyes like black stones, all bloodshot with hate and drink.

"Smart as a new sail, ain't yer?" he raved, and I could smell the rum on his breath. "Bright as brass, ye be, and hearty. Young ye are too, an' if we let ye live — which ain't 'tall likely — ye'll make one o' them dinky officers that gives all the orders. Years ye've got to make a fortune in, you swab. Maybe ye'll waste 'em, maybe ye'll have 'em stolen like mine was. Thirty year or more I spent livin' like a sewer rat; couldn't read nor write, spoke rough without any of them fancy haw-haws an' fancy manners that the magistrates fa-

34

vor. Halfpenny a day I got for holdin' horses or a penny a day helpin' chimney sweeps, an' lucky to get it."

He glared at me in an odd terrible way. I think he had a mind to say a lot more but Sweeney interrupted, nor was I sorry on that account.

"Do keep cool, don't lose your temper, Mr. Smiley," he said, wringing his hands. "It's gettin' dark, you know. We'll never make the Mariner at this rate."

"Stow it!" shouted Smiley turning on him. "Get them 'orses hitched up, you an' Gimp — go on, it was your idea takin' the coach in the first place."

"Always wanted me own coach," whined Sweeney. "Worth two 'undred pounds if it's worth a penny."

"Jump to it!" shouted Smiley in his ugly, angry voice, so full of hate.

"There'll be a hue and cry," grumbled Sweeney. "The Bosun will see to that."

"No more jaw," ordered Smiley. "Tie up this little devil's feet and throw 'im in the coach. You get in with 'im. Gimp ain't got brains enough to guard a rabbit 'utch."

Smiley gave me a fixed look fit to kill, while Sweeney tied my ankles. Then I was bundled into the coach, helpless as a trussed fowl. Never a word more did I say throughout these dismal proceedings, knowing full well that any protest would be useless and might provoke Smiley to such a degree that he would kill me then and there.

They left me and as they walked away I heard Smiley say something to the effect that I would be forced to sign articles for a good long voyage or else Deadlock would make an end of me since I knew too much and my tongue would need to be silenced somehow. Then I heard the horses being hitched up and it was a sorry, botched business judging by the arguments and swearing.

Sweeney being the one chosen to guard me, I had the benefit of his unsavory presence. Smiley took the coachman's seat while Gimp rode behind with one extra horse. What happened to the other I never discovered but I think the animal bolted.

The coach horses were still blown and tired, so what with a broken harness and a coach in need of a wheelwright, we made but poor time. But nonetheless we trundled forward, and there was I once again a passenger, though under much different circumstances than before. No longer was I a traveler in possession of a ticket, able to govern my own affairs and certain of my destination. Instead, I was a prisoner of desperate men, of pirates who would think nothing of killing me for a shilling piece should the need arise. Blunt had observed that I took the wrong coach and he uttered no truer words. Most fervently I wished, as I lay there with wrists and ankles tied, that I was back with honest Captain Campbell in his coasting brig.

A full moon, round as a pumpkin, had come up and by its silvery light I saw the grinning lantern-jawed Mr. Sweeney.

"Nasty situation for you, sir," he said. "Bad luck. Fate. No fault of yours bein' mixed up with Blunt. You shouldn't 'ave gone for old Gimp, though. Keep a cool 'ead at all times; only thing; pays in the long run."

"Mr. Sweeney, you are a murderer," said I. "There was

no need to kill the coachman. He likely had a wife and family. I'll see you swing for it."

"That's a lie, don't believe a word," said he hurriedly. "Not a one to speak 'gainst a man behind his back, I'm not, but it was Gimp, so it was. Good shot, Gimp. Regret it if the coachman died; likely in sin and without benefit of clergy."

"That's not something you'll need to worry about," said I. "You'll get all the preaching you want and all the rope you'll need, never fear."

"In a rare sour temper, ye are," said Sweeney, with a laugh. "I make allowance for it, bless yer 'eart. Better not talk back to Smiley, though. Almost 'ad yer on a lee shore. Nasty man is Smiley, rough as they come."

"And Deadlock, what of him?" I asked. "Who is he?"

"Best not to inquire," said Sweeney. "In trouble enough as it is. But I'll say this: 'e's a man who started 'umble, same as you. Not a one for backchat. Give 'im lip and there ye be, dead as Queen Anne."

"I'm dead anyway, by the looks of it," said I gloomily.

"Tut-tut, ye're broadside on but ye ain't struck yet," said he, with hideous cheerfulness. "Play yer cards well and off ye goes for a gentleman of fortune like the rest of us. Rich within a year, mark me words. I say, this is a rough stretch. Up and down like a butter churn."

We fell silent for a moment as the coach bounced from side to side. Smiley was good enough to set me easy in the opposite seat. Somehow I managed to wedge myself in the corner. He looked at me very shrewdly.

"Old Deadlock, he'll take to ye, Sonny," he said. "Some-thin' of a seaman, too, ain't ye? Ah, I could tell from the cut of yer jib. Always shorthanded, 'e is. Spirit, ye've got. I could tell that by the way ye went for Gimp."

Thus he rattled on and in return I was bound to tell a little of myself. What I didn't tell he asked after right out so that one way or another he had my name and some knowledge of my inclinations.

"Ah, ye'll be worth yer weight in gold afore long," said Sweeney admiringly. "Now yer take most common seamen (which you aint, that's clear), why they spends their money fast as they get it. Never a thought for the future. But you ain't like that, not you. It'll be money in bank, never a penny spent foolishly. Most of us can't count the fingers on our own 'ands much less the guineas in our pockets. Rum ain't good for countin' either, I'll say that without fear of contradiction."

With this sentiment I agreed readily enough and told him so. He sighed, looking doleful.

"If only I had youth and book learnin' like you," he said. "Doctorin', is it? That means Latin and Greek up to the 'atch covers. Ah, 'e'll like that, will old Deadlock! Play yer cards well, like I told ye, and keep yer temper, that's all."

"Easier said than done, at least with me," said I balefully, feeling how the rope bit cruelly into my wrists.

"Quite rightly observed," he replied, "but you 'as to try just the same. Take me, for instance; ye wouldn't believe it but once I was worse than Smiley for bad temper. Why, 'e was a lamb alongside o' me. Now? Why, I'm as sweet-

38

tempered as one o' them angels in the Bible. I never get up-
set. Cool, I am — cool as a cucumber."

I was on the point of asking Sweeney what had caused this
miraculous change in his manners but before I could utter a
word the coach came to a sudden jolting halt. Then a voice
called out, in peremptory fashion, "Stand, or I'll fire!"

A second later came the sound of a shot. At last, I thought,
the hue and cry has finally been aroused and the coach is
now stopped by soldiers!

Sweeney, at the first sound of firing, had dropped to the
floor of the coach where he crouched like an ostrich, his hands
clasped about his head and in such a state of fright that his
moaning was pitiful to hear. Struggling to the window as
best I could, I looked out. I was just in time to see Gimp level
his musket. Before he could pull the trigger another shot
rang out. Gimp fell from his horse without so much as a
cry. Leaning further out, I saw, by the light of the moon,
another body lying on the ground. It was Smiley. A man
wearing a mask stood facing me with leveled pistols.

"Try to keep cool, Mr. Sweeney," I said. "We are held up
by a highwayman — and I rather think he's a better shot than
Mr. Gimp."

5

I Am Set Free
by a Highwayman

THE HIGHWAYMAN ordered me to come forward, leaving
any weapons in the coach, and to stand before him with my
arms raised above my head. His manner was brisk, his voice
in its tone bore a knife-edge of authority.

"No tricks," he said, waving a grim pistol at the fallen
Smiley, "no tricks, or you join your friends."

"Only a fine trick could make me do as you ask," said I,
"since I am bound hand and foot and cannot move."

"The devil you are!" he muttered, nudging his horse forward. "Turn around. Remember, I have a pistol at your
head."

The coach door opened behind me and I heard an excla-
mation of surprise. Then a knife cut the rope about my ankles.

"We'll leave your hands tied for the moment," said he.
"Step down."

Then he caught signt of Sweeney crouching on the floor
and poked at him with a pistol.

"And who, pray, is this?" he snapped, with cold disapproval. "Is this a coach full of lunatics?"

I told him briefly what had happened, how the pirates had attacked us and how our coachman had been shot down in cold blood.

"An interesting tale," he said. "You must be carrying the crown jewels. Well, the world has two rascals less to worry about, if I'm not mistaken."

Then he asked me who I was and where I was going and I told him in polite fashion a little of my affairs.

"Well, then, you had better see to these rascals if you are something of a sawbones," he said. "All life has flown, I'm afraid, but we'd better make sure. Mr. Sweeney, untie this fellow's hands at once — and be quick about it!"

All this time Sweeney had crouched, white of face, gazing into the ugly mouth of a pistol fixed unwaveringly at his head. He seemed incapable of speech but scuttled out of the coach and had me free in a moment.

"It's wretches like Mr. Sweeney who make honest men go in fear of their lives, and ruin trade," said the highwayman — most unfairly, I thought, considering his own shortcomings. But as soon as I was free, I examined the fallen, discovering — and it was no great surprise — how they were beyond help, and for better or worse had gone to their Maker.

We found a pointed spade or shovel in the boot of the coach, useful I suppose for such emergencies as mud or potholes, but it did service for grave-digging that night. Thus we laid the pirates to their final rest. The highwayman was

41

correct in all matters pertaining to this last ceremony and he asked if I had either a Bible or a Book of Common Prayer about me. I told him that I had a Bible among my belongings and he bade me get it out that he might read a service.

All this made a great impression on Sweeney. At the coach, as he helped me down with my box, he whispered to me. "'E's cool, 'e is. No half measures for 'im. Nothing slap-dash. He's wicked with them pistols but 'e's a gentleman, too, and reverent."

He was clearly awestruck, remarking that Gimp and Smiley were lucky not being "turned off" — as he put it — at Tyburn or Execution Dock.

"None o' that hymn singing or hark-angel stuff in them places," he whispered. "Their poor ghosts walk about restless, without a prayer bein' said over 'em — and I'd sooner have them two peaceful, if ye know what I mean."

I knew what he meant well enough.

The scene was eerie and strange beyond all description. There we stood about the graves in the pale moonlight, our heads bowed, listening to the masked highwayman as he read the twenty-third Psalm with great feeling. How he managed to read from my Bible I do not know, though the moon shed a fair light. In any case, whether he read it or recited from memory, the effect was sadly moving, having considerable effect on Sweeney who, I noticed, wiped a tear from his eye. Then, with the reciting of the Lord's Prayer, this melancholy event was brought to a close. He snapped the Bible shut and handed it back to me.

"Now then," he said briskly, "I want both of you to unhitch those poor tired horses — draw the coach into the trees first — they're not fit to work more this night."

He supervised the task, sitting, with pistols drawn, on a powerful-looking black mare. We knew better than to cross him. Mr. Blunt's tin box was removed, the contents ransacked by the highwayman, though what he discovered of value I had no way of knowing at the time — and cared less.

When we had at last done with the coach, he ordered me to mount the late Mr. Smiley's horse. This I did without a word, balancing my box as best I could before me. He then ordered Sweeney to take Gimp's old horse.

"Now, Mr. Sweeney, you will do as I say," he ordered grimly, "or you will repent, make no mistake. Time is running short. Soon the revenue men will be out looking for the coach — and for you. If they find you, why, you'll swing for certain. That you know well enough. Have you any money?"

"Oh, very little, sir," whined Sweeney. "It's good of you to ask, sir, so it is. I has a sixpence here and there, but nothin' as would cause me to live high, sir."

The highwayman tossed him a small leather purse. "Here you are then," he said, "as next of kin. All I discovered on your friends."

Sweeney's eyes opened wide. "If ye think it right, sir," he said, in a sort of whisper.

"I do. I need you independent of the world for a time," said the highwayman. "You have money. You have a mount.

A mile along this road you will come to a crossroads. Can you read?"

"Quite well, sir."

"Good. The signpost will point to the Bristol road. This you will take. Once in Bristol you know what to do."

"Oh, yes, sir," said Sweeney eagerly. "I'll find a vessel, sir, depend on it. Goin' anywhere, sir."

"And don't let me set eyes on you again," said the highwayman, "or you'll regret it. I warn you, Sweeney, I have ways of finding out — secret ways. I have a long arm. You'll discover it to your cost if you disregard my orders. Do you understand?"

"Oh, yes, indeed, sir, every blessed word," answered Sweeney, with such a degree of fervor that I had no doubt that, for the moment, the pirate meant what he said.

He left us then, but the masked man watched, muttering under his breath, until Sweeney vanished up the moonlit road. Then he turned to me, saying that I had best accompany him to the next town where he knew of a place to stay the night. The landlord, he said, was a loyal friend and would be sure to look after my every need — including a coach seat to Plymouth, because the Dolphin was a posting inn for coaches along that route.

"I shall be glad of that," said I. "Plymouth is a place I should very much like to see."

He laughed. "Never fear, Mr. Carruthers, you will get there eventually. Now I think we must be on our way — and as quickly as we can."

45

Now you must understand that I was quite at a loss to know what had best be done. I was betwixt and between whether to stay with this rascal or pursue my journey, even if he should allow it, for he was armed and I was not. Furthermore, I was penniless, since all my small wealth had been stolen by the pirates, indeed given to Sweeney by this same rascal who, no doubt, was always generous with other people's money. Also, rascal or not, he had certainly released me from the pirates and to that extent I was in his debt.

We had traveled only a short distance, perhaps a quarter of a mile, when the matter was settled with great suddenness and beyond all argument when a clatter of hoofbeats drew rapidly toward us. The highwayman gave me a push.

"Quickly, into the trees," he said quietly, at the same time drawing his pistols.

Obedient but sullen I nudged my horse off the road into the dark shadows of a little grove of tall pines just as a party of horsemen swept by.

How I longed to hail them! Brave fellows! Here truly was rescue, and rescue galloped past within a stone's throw while I skulked there like a common thief. How bitterly I now cursed my fate, how desperately I wanted to dash out, to take my place once more in the world of free men! But alas! the highwayman kept not only a hand on the bridle of my horse but also a pistol not too far away from my heart.

They were past us in a moment, like a charge of cavalry. Then, as we stood there beneath the trees, there came a shout, the galloping stopped — and I knew the coach had been discovered.

"If you please, I rather think I should reveal my presence to those men," said I desperately.

"Oh no, you will not," he growled. "I'll not allow it. You do as I say or suffer the consequences." He then pointed to a little path that wound among the trees.

"Off you go, my lad, and no nonsense," he said. "I'm just as sorry about this as you are. Watch your step and be quiet. Any tricks and you're finished. Now remember."

There was nothing for it but to obey. Seething with anger, I nonetheless walked my horse (or the late Mr. Smiley's horse, if you will) along the narrow path, conscious of his pistols at my back and flinching at every crack of a twig.

On and on we journeyed, without a word being said. Frequently my face was slashed by branches that overhung the path and I soon learned to keep my head down. Also as we entered more deeply into the wood, the path became more difficult to discern so that we rather felt our way forward than knew for certain our direction. But suddenly the trees thinned and we stood on the edge of a clearing, flooded with moonlight. He whispered that I must halt and came up beside me, listening intently, but all I heard was the hooting of an owl and the night wind whispering in the trees.

"You flatter yourself if you believe I would raise the countryside because of you, sir!" said I, breathing hard with rage. "Believe it or not, I have better things to do. You're safe enough for the time being — as safe as you'll likely be till

47

the sun comes up. If you don't mind, I wish to be on my way."

"You keep quiet!" he said fiercely. "You talk too much for a young lad. A regular chatterbox, you are."

Despair gripped me now as well as rage.

"You can go to the devil in your own way," said I. "Not a step farther will I go with you."

"You'll do as you're told," he said wearily, "or I'll blow your silly brains out. Think I'm going to let you wander into the hands of the Revenue — or the Squire? Not bloomin' likely! I'll bide my time and let you off when it pleases me. Not before!"

Well, I thought, he has ideas of letting me go eventually. Meanwhile I would exercise what small patience I possessed. Indeed under the circumstances I had no alternative. Therefore, I sat in my saddle, thinking my own dark thoughts; sullen, angry, but keeping as good a rein on my tongue as I could muster.

He removed his bicorn hat — a beautiful velvet thing trimmed with silver cord — and fanned the midges that flew about our heads.

"I'm sorry to put you out of countenance," he said, almost cheerfully. "But there it is; it can't be helped. You'll be wise to make the best of it."

6

A Fight at the Crossroads

He made no further remark but sat there on his black horse, listening for any sign of pursuit. Then, in a low voice, he told me to dismount and we led our horses across a little field. I think a farm or country cottage was somewhere about for I heard a dog bark a long way off and he stopped to listen. But soon all became quiet again and we continued on our way.

We picked a careful path through a small grove of ancient stately trees and crossed a little muttering brook, all lively in the moonlight. This place, he told me in subdued tones, was the far border of a great estate, a duke's property, though it looked lonely enough to be a wilderness at the world's edge.

On we traipsed, coming at last to a moor, a gloomy stretch of rolling land covered with turf and short grass, very coarse, with ugly whitish stones scattered all about. The place reminded me of stone-age men, of heathenish customs and human sacrifices, nor was I exactly pleased when my companion expressed a wish to rest and talk and let the horses crop their supper by the wayside. He pleased me, however, by taking a leather pouch from the saddle and sharing with me the meal of bread and cheese that it contained, for I was famished almost beyond endurance.

We sat opposite, each on a small boulder. The moon still rode high but now a wind sprang up, chilling to the bone. He began then to question me closely, asking who I was, where I came from and what trade I followed. I told him more of my ambitions to be a surgeon, that I had spent only a year at my studies before my uncle had passed away. About the voyage I gave a full account, also about Mr. Blunt and his leaping from the coach. He questioned me in a careful, calculating way about The Bosun, from the time I first saw him on the brig until the final dramatic parting.

When I had finished he seemed, for some reason, satisfied, even relieved, though for what cause I could not imagine. Then he took off his mask and wiped his face with a kerchief. With some curiosity I looked at him as he sat there in the moonlight. I saw that he was dark, with eyes that were narrow and keen, his mouth set in lines of firm determination. There was altogether a look of recklessness about him and yet of calculation also, so that he appeared at once daring and shrewd. It crossed my mind that here was a man of great courage, and yet a man mindful of the pitfalls of this world, quite ready to take a chance if the stakes were only high enough. He put the mask in his pocket against the time, I supposed, when it would be needed.

Shuddering now with the cold, I grew restless and impatient.

"Well, Mr. Highwayman," I said, "you and I cannot stay this way forever. I thank you for your help. I'll carry no tales."

"And do I have your honest word for that?" he asked.

"Yes," said I, "and my hand upon it, too."

"Then it's a bargain," said he, looking serious. We shook hands and after that no more was said on the subject. Thus, quite suddenly, our relationship changed. While I could not easily forget his violent ways, nonetheless I recognized his courage. Reckless he was, without a doubt, but he was also kind when it pleased him. He came, I thought, from a better part of society than his present occupation seemed to indicate. Certainly he spoke well and seemed a man of good education so that, all in all, he was a puzzle to me. But I knew better than to delve into matters that did not concern me — nor did I care that much, being only anxious to go, once more, about my own business.

But to my surprise the less I inquired about his affairs the more he seemed willing to reveal. His trust, once given, was given wholeheartedly, without stint or reserve. We had resumed our journey toward the town, being now less than two miles from Moorefields where, I thought, all my troubles would end. As we walked along leading our horses, he told me that I might call him Matthew, that he was by trade a printer and that he had been arrested for printing a tract unfavorable to the King. As punishment he had suffered transportation to Australia but had escaped and now chose to earn his "living," as he called it, by highway piracy.

"Mind you," he said, "I printed nothing that wasn't true. But the bigger the truth, the greater the crime. If you choose to cross swords with power, my boy, you have to take the consequences."

"You were treated overharshly," I said, feeling real sympathy for him. "Where's freedom if a man can't speak his true mind on occasion?"

"Ah, where indeed?" he said. "Take this war for instance; where's truth now? Dead as a doornail, the first casualty. A plain man daren't say a word."

By this time the weather had undergone a change. A gusty wind drove clouds across the moon; the light was reluctant and fitful: on one minute, and off the next. We had arrived almost to the heath's edge. Ahead lay the road to Moorefields, the ground sloping upward, not sharply but with a gentle rise. I remember glancing ahead even while Matthew was talking and I saw a finger post, looking remarkably like a gallows, outlined against the night sky. The next moment — and I gulped with fright — I saw the outline of several horsemen gathered there.

"Matthew, we must be careful," I whispered, tugging his sleeve. "If we move another step we shall be discovered."

Silently, without a word, he led both horses to a spot behind a group of boulders, not large enough to hide us entirely but tolerable cover and better than nothing.

"We may be discovered already," he whispered grimly. "If I'm caught I'm a dead man. Are you all right on a fast horse?"

"I ride well enough," I said quietly.

"This is no place to hide," he whispered irritably. "If they don't see us, why, they must be blind."

He pressed a pistol into my hand.

"Take it," he whispered. "One shot may save your skin. You never know."

I took it, feeling vastly pleased by this token of his confidence and trust.

"We act like guilty men," said I. "They may see us but not care. Perhaps you imagine trouble."

"I only hope you're right," he whispered. "We'll know soon enough."

We peered into the night, barely moving, hoping against hope that the horses would remain quiet. The men were outlined against the moon, half a dozen at least. I could hear a faint murmur of voices and the rattle of the harness bits as the animals tossed their heads.

And then the moon went in, leaving everything as dark as a pit. By the time it had struggled out again the men were gone.

"What did I tell you," said I, after we had waited a cautious moment. "They didn't see us. Friends returning home, nothing more."

"Not so fast, dear boy," said he. "A good half hour we'll give 'em as a head start."

He sighed. Our horses munched the miserable short grass that grew among the stones.

"I don't much care for this," he said. "I don't like it at all."

"They made no move against us," said I. "In any case, what can we do, we can't stay here all night?"

"Aye, you're right," he grumbled. "We'll have to continue on regardless. Perhaps I'm overcautious. But it's well enough for you. There's no stain on your character with the squires and magistrates. They would just as soon hang me as look at me."

"Give me time," I said. "They may hang me yet." I told him then that I proposed going by myself into the town of Moorefields and there find out what I could regarding our situation.

"There'll be news at the inn — the Dolphin — I think you said; also I'll buy us food," said I.

"And that's sensible," said he. "At least you'll hear news of that wretch Sweeney. Damn him! If they catch the fellow there's no knowing what stories he'll tell. He's no man to trust. Ah, I should have done for him, once and for all." He swore again and muttered under his breath.

"But I'm not a one to dispatch in cold blood," he said, with a sigh. "Not even my worst enemies. It's what you'd call a weakness of spirit. I'll likely pay dearly for it before I'm done."

"A weak spirit is not something you suffer from overmuch," said I, remembering the two graves freshly dug only an hour since.

"If you're thinking of the pirates," he said, "I only defended myself. A man has an obligation to save his own life. Snuffed me out like a candle, they would — and you, too, without a second thought. Here we are. Be careful now."

We climbed to the road. There was the signpost pointing to Moorefields. Nearby a footpath, dimly seen, led away

54

to a dark wood. He told me that he knew of a deserted cottage there.

"Follow the path," he said. "You can see it plain enough. Follow it until you come to a great oak. You can't fail to see it. I'm sure old King Alfred must have planted it, it's that big. Stand under it and whistle — let me see — yes, whistle the first bar or two of 'John Peel.' I'll wait for you until morning."

He dabbed his forehead with a kerchief and put on his fine bicorn hat. Then he held out his hand.

"Good-by, dear boy," he said gravely. "Fortune or circumstance may prevent your return. Who knows?"

"Within the hour," I said firmly, "I shall return, with food and with news."

He shook his head. "Nothing's certain in this world, Steve. If you turn up, well and good. I'll appreciate the food. I'll be a mite hungry, no doubt. But if you're not back by cockcrow, why then I'll be off. These parts aren't safe for me."

"Will you take my box?" I asked. "It's a fair hindrance to riding."

He took it with a faint smile. "You'll know where to find it if I'm gone," he said. And then, with a whispered "Good luck to you, Steve!" his black horse trotted along the little path and vanished into the trees.

Wasting no time I turned my own horse in the direction of Moorefields. Four miles, the signpost had said, a fair distance, particularly at night on a strange road. As the animal trotted along I let my thoughts dwell on my peculiar situation. Here I was, riding a dead man's horse and in league with

55

a highwayman! The devil take it! How could reason justify my continuing the arrangement? Now that I was free of Matthew I could do as I pleased. He had no claim on me. I could reach the Dolphin, stay the night and leave for Plymouth on the morning coach — without my box, of course, and I cursed myself for a fool in letting him take it. All my worldly goods were in it — my clothes, a few books, and my late uncle's telescope. This last I valued above everything else and the thought of losing it made my heart sink.

Grown now mighty irritable, I gave up musing on my queer misfortunes and looked about me, leaning a little forward to see what I could of the road. One pothole might have serious consequences, nor did I relish the possibility of being thrown or the horse made lame.

For some time I journeyed thus, on the lookout for such perils of the road as might harm the beast that carried me. Alas, I had no eyes for other darker perils, perils that hid among the long black shadows of the trees.

Before me stretched a dismal avenue of pines and I remember how carefully I rode. The way at this point was so dark that little could be seen. So, potholes or not, we jogged along with me peering ahead, talking irritably to myself. Through this gloomy avenue I went, as I say, and came at last to the end. Directly ahead, in a splash of moonlight, I could see the crossroads and a fingerpost, while beyond I glimpsed a light from the window of an outlying house of Moorefields.

I had just given a nudge to my horse to go faster when suddenly the beast reared. I heard a shout and before I could so much as draw my pistol I was surrounded, dragged from my horse and thrown to the ground.

Somehow I managed to regain my feet and for a short time made a real fight of it, planting my knee heavily in someone's belly and my fist on someone's nose, this with such good effect that I heard a howl of pain. The scene was a melee of plunging horses and shouting, angry men. But the melancholy fact was that I was at last subdued, my arms held by two burly revenue officers and we all stood looking at each other, panting, swearing and angry as wild dogs.

7

My Encounter with the Squire

A LANTERN APPEARED from somewhere and was held up before me.

"I trust the sport was to your liking," said I, breathing hard. "Attacking a lawful traveler, taking his horse — this is new work for the King's men!" I glared back at their peering, hostile faces. One officer, I was pleased to note, held a kerchief to a bloody nose, and another, his eye half closed and swollen, shook a fist at me.

"What's your name, boy?" growled the man with the lantern.

"Bonnie Prince Charlie!" I said. "I'll not answer your questions!"

"Insolent fellow!" cried a large portly man standing beside the lantern-bearer.

"Insolent fellow, a ruffian if ever I saw one! You will answer Major Baxter's questions. Great violence has been done in this parish. A coach, a royal mail coach, has been grievously attacked and robbed. A royal mail coach, sir, think of it — and in this parish!"

His jowls shook with indignation. Well, he had good cause to be indignant. I was not prepared to argue the point and told him so. I also stated that if I was treated with some regard for the rights of a free man, why, then I would be willing, nay, eager, to answer any reasonable questions they cared to ask.

"Well enough put, I think," said the lantern-bearer, looking sideways at the portly gentleman.

"Release him, but watch him closely!" snapped Portly. "He's obviously not to be trusted. Fighting and punching the revenue officers — loyal men only doing their duty — I'll not have it! Now, sir, your name and place of abode!"

Of course I told him: from Scotland by way of Nova Scotia. He nodded ponderously.

"Then you are not native to these shores?"

"Well, no," I said. "Not strictly speaking."

"Fact number one," he said, closing his eyes. "The prisoner is not native to these shores. Is that your horse?" He pointed a finger at the gray, now quietly chewing nettles by the wayside.

"Yes," I said, with some hesitation, and most unwisely as matters turned out. In a sense the animal was mine, if only by right of damages, or even perhaps by right of salvage. But in all truth the horse belonged to a dead man — and I shrank, like any coward, from the pitfalls of that wretched history. How close disaster hung upon my words!

"Yes, that's my horse," I said firmly and without a blush.

"Fact number two," said the portly man, closing his eyes.

"The prisoner admits to owning a certain gray horse. Major Baxter, have a man search the saddlebag."

Saddlebag! What saddlebag? A most horrid dread now presented itself. What saddlebag indeed! There it had been, next to my knee, and I paying no more attention to it than a fly. Had I felt it? Nay, rather ask if I had time or opportunity to feel or consider anything beyond preserving life and sanity. I cursed my negligence and hoped. What a hope!

An officer quickly unbuckled the flap. In went his hand. Out came a bundle tied securely with string.

"And what have we here?" said the portly one, his jowls trembling with anticipation.

"Mail, I fancy, if you please, sir," said the officer. "Valuable mail by the looks of it. String unbroken and seals in place, sir."

"Valuable mail, seals in place," repeated old Portly closing his eyes. He put out a large, chubby hand. "Give it to me at once," he said.

I watched as he ripped off paper, seals and string. I saw him open a cardboard box and peer inside. Then, without a word or any noticeable change of expression, he handed it back to the officer.

"We are not interested in birds eggs," he said, "however valuable they may be. Search the coach; rip it to pieces if need be. We must find it." Then he looked at me and my heart sank to my boots.

"Mail in your saddlebag, Mr. Carruthers. Odd, most odd. Have you a reasonable explanation — a license perhaps from the King? A little private contract with the Revenue Office to carry the mails?"

He paused heavily and, I can tell you, it was my turn to close my eyes and to think with vast concentration.

"Fact number three," he intoned. "The prisoner has valuable mail in his saddlebag, and can proffer no reasonable explanation for same."

His words brought me to my senses, to a full understanding of my awful predicament. I must tell the full story, and devil take the consequences, if any, to Matthew. To him I owed but little. And there would be no need to reveal his hiding place. In that regard alone I owed him loyalty. My mind was made up.

"Quite incorrect," I said. "There is a reasonable explanation for all this. To begin with, that horse is not mine, nor is the saddlebag. I know nothing of anything you may find there."

He looked at me in blank astonishment. Then he closed his eyes, as if in pain.

"Are you trying to tell me, sir, that the same horse you claimed a moment ago — claimed, I might say, with unhesitating firmness — are you, sir, now denying that claim?"

Wearily I said, "Yes, sir, I am."

"One minute you own a horse, the next minute you don't. Is that it? Should I say rather, that now we have discovered stolen property on said horse, property only lately come from a certain mail coach, now that we have discovered it, I say — you now find it convenient to deny ownership of the animal?"

Major Baxter had been looking at me with interest and attention. He frowned, remarking that nothing was yet proven regarding the mail.

"It may be just as well to let the boy have his head, sir, if I may say so. We can't stand here all night. Tell your story, boy. You have nothing to fear if you tell the truth."

Thus encouraged, I told my story, from the time I left Glasgow to the last desperate moments in the coach. The major followed every word with unswerving attention. When I had done, he said that my tale had the ring of truth to it since nothing in it was believable as fiction.

"Well I for one don't believe a word of it!" said old Portly. "Major Baxter, you're too soft and credulous by far. The young ruffian is a liar. He's already lied about the horse. He's to be locked up till next assizes. We'll deal with him then!"

At these words, so unfair and so completely unjust, all my recent misfortune seemed to boil up as it were, like a volcano. Sad it is to relate that I lost my temper utterly and completely. In short, I hit the fellow in that region of the waistcoat where his waist should have been. He toppled over backward into the straining arms of two revenue men. They were considerate enough to lower him gently to the ground, where he lay, gasping and groaning like a stranded whale.

"That's the Squire you've hit," exclaimed Major Baxter with dismay. "Good heavens, boy, what are you thinking of?" He was exceedingly angry, saying that my behavior would get me nowhere except into more hot water. Then he ordered me to accompany him to Moorefields where I was to

63

be lodged at the Dolphin and there kept under guard until morning. As for the Squire, he left us, accompanied by two officers, and as he rode past, I saw his face in the lamplight and the look he gave me boded ill for the future.

Thus I was bundled off, Major Baxter on one side and a tall revenue man carrying a musket on the other. Behind us, all mounted and in single file, came the balance of the company so that my entry into the sleepy village proved as imposing as that of a captured Napoleon.

Subdued though I now was regarding my treatment of the Squire — a man who had the power to do me much harm — I had lost but little of my anger. As we marched along, Baxter carrying his candle-lantern, I protested my innocence once again, telling him that he and his precious Squire would pay dearly for their mistake once the real truth was known.

"That may be," he said, "but the roads are not safe for peaceful travelers. Highwaymen have been far too active in these parts and it's got to stop. Here I find you on the road at a late hour with stolen mail. Fishy, I call it, damn fishy. I would be doing less than my duty not to put you under lock and key until inquiries are made — and inquiries will be made, depend upon it."

All this sounded so horribly reasonable that my heart sank. I asked him if I might be allowed to send a letter to my old friend, Captain Mullins, at Plymouth.

"I'll promise nothing," he snapped. "You'll be facing Squire Jenkyns in the morning. You can ask him."

From that moment I kept silent, but my thoughts were smoldering like a hayrick by the time we came to Moorefields. He did, however, apologize for the lack, as he put it, of "suitable accommodation" for prisoners since the village was small and crime rare.

"Instead we pay a fee to the landlord of the Dolphin," he explained, "a Mr. Wells. He's a rough man if you play tricks but fair enough otherwise."

The inn was dark and shut fast when we arrived but Mr. Wells, a short, hairy, humpbacked man, very sinister to look at, came down in answer to the Major's banging on the door.

"Squire's business, Mr. Wells, if you please," said he. The whole miserable affair was then explained to the landlord, who all the while yawned and scratched his head.

"If he's not dangerous, I'll keep him here the night," said he. "But I'll not be responsible. You'll supply an armed guard, I hope. Ale for the guard is included, but no supper for the prisoner." He looked me over with such piercing eyes that I felt somehow guilty of all the crimes in Christendom.

"Highwayman, is it? Well now, it's a sad pity — a fine-looking fellow like you. Tut-tut, what would your mother say, I wonder!"

"A mistake has been made, if you don't mind," I grated between my teeth. "I'm no highwayman. But if I ever meet that overfed wretch you call a Squire on a dark night — "

"Now, now," snapped Major Baxter. "You do yourself more harm by such talk!"

Mr. Wells stared at me. "If Squire Jenkyns says you're a highwayman, why then a highwayman you are," he said.

This last remark was so final and likely so true that little remained except to lock me up. In short, this most melancholy part of my history ended with my imprisonment in a storage room for empty wine barrels and other oddments. Into this I was cast and the heavy oak door locked and bolted. Airless, windowless, the place was a home for spiders, earwigs and countless mice that scurried about, squeaking and rustling among the rubbish.

My anger had now given way to a vast weariness. Feeling about I came upon a pile of sacks in a corner. Casting myself upon them I fell, almost immediately, into a deep sleep.

8

Trapped in the Old Mill

I was awakened by the hunchback, Mr. Wells, who poked at me with an old-fashioned bell-mouthed blunderbuss. He stood over me, candle in hand, his great ugly shadow trembling on the wall.

"Up you get, son," he said in a loud whisper. "I want a word with you."

Wearily, sleepily protesting, I sat up, then staggered to my feet. In a daze I stumbled outside. A guard slept on the floor, propped up against the wall near the door. The hunchback placed a finger to his lips, motioning with the blunderbuss for me to walk ahead. He had the goodness to guide me down a series of curved steps made of stone and, passing through a heavy iron-studded door at the bottom, we came to the cellar of the inn. Here were stored the barrels of rum and wine; bottles by the hundred dozen reached to the ceiling in long racks. It was a place of dust and cobwebs and yet of vague pleasant smells too.

He lit a three-pronged candlestick, setting it on a long pine table that ran along one side of the room. Because of the blunderbuss, which he kept snugly tucked under his arm, his movements were necessarily restricted and I noted how he always managed to keep between us an obstacle of furniture, that is a chair, the table or great barrel of wine. But while he kept a handy finger near the trigger, he spoke kindly enough, bidding me sit at the table and eat a meal of sliced ham and rich dark bread that I found spread before me. I needed no second bidding. Fully awake now, I ate like a wolf, paying no more attention to manners than a savage.

Before I had quite finished, he asked me to tell my story.

"This is surprising," said I, "since you heard it all from Major Baxter."

"Nay, I'm no fool," he said. "You have a different tale to tell, I fancy."

Well, I had, true enough, and I told it, from the time I left Glasgow to the last desperate moments in the coach. I told about the highwayman, the slaying and burial of the two pirates, and my final capture by the Revenue. When I had done, he asked shrewdly after Matthew, though not by name. I put him off, saying I did not think it right or proper to discuss the highwayman or his comings or goings. His black eyes gleamed like jet beads in the candlelight.

"This man, whoever he is, will verify and prove your account of the affair. Betray him to the Squire and you are saved. Without his evidence, you are lost. The Squire will not take your word alone. It's too much to expect."

"Devil take the Squire!" I burst out. "I'll not betray the man to save my own skin. He may well be a rascal, but he has more courage in his little finger than all your wretched squires put together. He saved me from a pack of murderers.

The least I can do in return is to hold my tongue. No, I'll not betray the man, stranger to me though he is."

"Then you may lose your life," he said. "You are certain to lose your liberty."

"It's a risk I am willing to take," said I, "and my own business after all."

"As to that," he returned, "it's not your business entirely. Others are involved, whether you like it or no." His manner was calm and collected, as if he knew a great deal more than he was willing to reveal. Taken aback I stared at him.

It crossed my mind suddenly that Mr. Wells had been testing my loyalty to the highwayman, that all this talk was only meant to sound me out. I was much on the alert then, and even had an inkling of what was to come.

"I believe this highwayman you speak of is known to me," he continued. "Nay, he's more than that. If his name is Matthew he is my brother's son. He is my nephew. My brother was killed in the wars many years ago."

"He calls himself Matthew," I said, staring at him. I saw the same dark hair and eyes, the same set to the mouth.

"Then he's undoubtedly the one," said he. "I just wanted to make sure. You can understand that I feel an obligation toward him. But, the knowledge of this relationship is a secret. If the news got abroad I'd be a ruined man — particularly with the Squire."

"You may depend on me, sir," said I. "Only his first name is known to me. I have no curiosity regarding his last. As for the Squire, I rather think he has a skeleton or two in his own cupboard."

He looked at me quickly. "What makes you say that?" he asked.

"Nothing much," said I, "but he seems overly anxious about the mail coach, no less so than the pirates were. One thing he has in common with them."

"And what is that?" said he.

"They all appear to be looking for something — something rather valuable. There's a smell of money about it — and death too."

He sighed and turned away.

"There's a war on, you know," he said, "and strange things happen. Jenkyns is one of the higher-ups and there's a deal of coming and going that we don't know about."

"Even so, I don't like it," said I.

"But you see, he's the Squire," said the hunchback. "Folk hereabouts are inclined to judge a man by his name. My ancestors were not exactly law-abiding, I can tell you that much."

"You likely pay your debts," said I.

"Yes," said he, "but it's not the debts I worry about, it's the credit." There was a look of sadness in his face when he turned away.

"I also have a child," he said. "A bad name is a hard thing for a child to bear." He sighed again. "But enough," he continued. "I have a favor to ask, and the doing of it may save you."

"I am a prisoner," I said. "In a few hours I must face the Squire."

"I put it to you," said he, "you may leave here immediately, if you care to run the risks of a fugitive."

"It's a risk either way," I said, "whether I go or stay."

"Very true," he said. "But if I let you go, I must have your word that you will warn my nephew. Warn him to flee the country. The bailiffs and revenue men watch every cross-roads, every inn, every important coach. You saw how it was last night."

"You have my word," I said. "I know where he is. But he knows his danger well enough."

"It is above all vitally important that you warn him against using a certain old house in Hawksley forest," he said. "The Squire has suspicions regarding it. Matthew must not go near the place on any account."

"Hawksley forest?" I whispered in a sort of daze. "The old house? Why, Mr. Wells, he's there now."

Speechless we stared at each other, then the hunchback told me to follow him.

"We only waste precious time," he said, his lips trembling with anguish. "You must be away from here!"

I followed as he directed, my thoughts in a turmoil by this swift change of fortune. One minute I was a helpless prisoner, well on the road to some terrible oblivion, the next I was offered, like a bird, the open door of my cage.

"Watch your head," said he. "This is a back entry. I find it useful on occasion."

We came to a door leading to a grain shed, where sacks of oats and corn were kept. We hurried through to come out at last upon the outside, where all was dark and silent. Mr. Wells took one candle from the sconce, snuffing the rest. Then I followed him across a flagstoned open space and thence

behind the big stable to a grassy plot or small paddock. Here, in the dimness, I saw my horse already saddled and waiting. I climbed up without a word.

"There is a lane," he said pointing. "It leads to the road you came by."

He then handed me a pistol, also powder and ball, and this I was glad to have because Matthew's pistol had been taken from me by Major Baxter.

"Take this also," he said, handing me a package. "It's bread and cheese and good hunks of meat."

Quickly I stuffed this into a side pocket of my coat. Then I bent down and shook his hand.

"Good luck, my friend," he whispered, "and God be with you both."

Thus we parted, the horse trotting quietly up the soft dirt lane. Once I had gained the main road I urged the animal forward and we flew along like the wind. Only once did I look back. There was the inn sign on its post, dark against the sky, a sky now faintly luminous with early dawn.

The dawn, the sun, my enemy! Would I be the first to reach Matthew, or were the Squire and his men already closing in on the lonely cottage? I dug in my heels so that my poor beast, without knowing, ran a race with the sun. How swiftly we galloped full tilt along that dark and lonely road, quite heedless of potholes or of anything or anyone that might stand in our way! The dust flew in clouds behind; the wind drove the hair back from my forehead.

Presently the first trees of Hawksley forest loomed in front. I reigned in my sweating, foaming horse, to trot at a more reasonable pace until we reached the old signpost — the fateful gallows signpost pointing to Moorefields. From there I soon discovered the footpath. Dismounting, I led my horse into the forest until we came at last to the great oak tree described by Matthew. All was quiet as I stood there beneath its huge, spreading, ancient arms. And then from a long way off a cock crowed and it was morning.

With, I thought, considerable feeling for the notes, I began to whistle "John Peel" and with the first bar a rabbit bounded away into the underbrush close by. This sudden movement so alarmed me that my concert ended almost before it began. But I had no need to continue. From behind the vast trunk of the oak came Matthew and the black mare.

"Where have you been, dear boy?" he said, looking serious and unsmiling. "I was about to leave."

"And you had better, as quickly as you can!" said I, and then I told him briefly of my encounter with the Squire and the revenue men and the meeting with his uncle, Mr. Wells, and the latter's warning about the cottage.

"The trap was almost sprung," he said grimly, "but the revenue men were not exactly quiet as mice. They almost battered down the front door. I left rather hurriedly by the back way, not ten minutes since. Come on, we've little time before the sun comes above the trees."

The air shimmered with gray light and birds began twittering among the boughs. Cautiously, we trod the forest path, leading our horses, walking in single file. If there was now a measure of daylight, there was also fear because of it. I stared at every bush, every fallen tree, expecting at any moment to hear the deadly crack of a musket or angry shout of the Squire's men. What we did hear finally was neither man nor gun but something in a way more alarming.

We had stopped to listen and my heart was in my mouth when I heard, from a little way off, the deep-throated baying of dogs. I came up to stand beside Matthew.

"They sound uncommonly bloodthirsty," he murmured, his shrewd eyes glancing at every shadowy place. "If they come after us with dogs it's an insult I'll not likely forget. I'll fight for the French." His mood was ugly.

"It might be a fox hunt," I whispered nervously. "Yesterday we passed through a duke's park. It can't be far away."

"Possibly," he grumbled. "The question is, does the duke hunt foxes with four legs or two?"

Fearing the worst I said nothing and we moved on, walking side by side now since the path had become much wider. The dogs seemed to draw closer by every passing minute.

"He'll be having fine sport, by the sound of it," remarked Matthew presently. "There's open country ahead, before we reach the coast road — and a hunted fox is not partial to open country."

The road continued to improve and I saw the wheel marks of a heavy cart. We took to the saddle then, proceeding thus at a fair pace until we came at last to the very edge of the forest. In front was an open place that caught the early morning sun.

"There's a choice to be made now," said Matthew. "Abandon the horses and reenter the forest, or make a run for it."

I thought the forest a trap if we stayed in it and told him

so. He said that I was likely right and besides, letting the horses go would be a great calamity. Hurriedly we made up our minds; the baying of the hounds now close at hand, acted on our wits like a spur. Galloping into open country, the sun now fairly up and dew still on the grass, we saw a little stream. Not far off, on the opposite bank, stood an ancient mill, and grazing nearby were three horses. I could see how Matthew took all this in at a glance.

"Come," he shouted, "we'll beat them yet!"

Furiously we galloped to the stream, Matthew on his black mare took the jump like a bird but my poor beast would have none of it and walked carefully through the shallow water. Impatient and fearful, I glanced back toward the forest but saw as yet no visible evidence of the wretched dogs, though I heard enough from them to wake the dead.

Once across the stream I joined Matthew, now hidden behind the mill. He was at work taking off the saddle and in urgent tones bade me do the same with mine. I obeyed at once. Never was harness removed from a horse with such speed; within moments both animals were free, grazing with their new companions as if they belonged there.

Meanwhile, Matthew and I entered the old mill by means of a door still in good repair but with hinges that shrieked in agony when we closed it. Even as the first dogs ran across the field we managed, by dint of much grunting and pushing, to drive home the rusty old bolt. The enemy, I thought, will have as little chance of getting past this door as we of getting out. We secured also the main entry by forcing it shut and dropping a bar of iron into slots across the panels so that nothing less than a battering ram would ever open it from the outside.

Thus in that gloomy, echoing place we stood, looking warily about, safe for the moment from dogs, squires and revenue men. From windows and cracks in the old brickwork shone narrow beams of sunlight, alive with moving dust. The massive wooden shaft of the mill wheel loomed above our heads, and outside, hugging the wall, was the great wheel itself, silent and still these many years. At one time the stream that gave it power had perhaps run faster or deeper, or the milling of flour had been a more profitable enterprise. But whatever the reason, the mill had stood derelict since Cromwell's day. The big wooden cogs that once obeyed the driving power of moving water were now a mass of cobwebs. Even as I looked, a yellow butterfly entered by an unshuttered window, to flit above the vagrant weeds that grew from every crevice of the heavy millstones. Bats hung from the rafters and timid mice found sanctuary beneath the floor.

A beam of light fell on the lower steps of a staircase. Quickly, and with but a look passed between us, we ascended, finding that the old wood groaned under our tread. But the steps held and once at the top we discovered yet another room, this with a ladder to a trapdoor in the ceiling. I tested the rungs and climbed, pushing on the door to find it give way with surprising ease. I clambered over the dusty sill; a moment later Matthew had joined me in this topmost room, the attic chamber of the mill. The ladder was drawn up from below and the trapdoor shut. By wedging ladder against door and roof our attic was now safe from sudden invasion.

I could hear the dogs now as they ran all about the mill and thought grimly that if they should discover us, our enemies would only need to wait patiently for our surrender or our death since we had but little food and no water. A siege, if it came, would be a short one, for thirst and hunger must surely defeat us in the end.

9

Unwelcome Visitors

Shutters covered the small opening of a window, but light, escaping through cracks in the boards, lit the attic tolerably well. Peeping through, we could see the eager, panting dogs far below, also a number of horsemen, six at least, moving about on the opposite bank.

A horrid thought came to me. "The saddles!" I cried. "Where did we leave them?"

"All safe below," said Matthew, "in a place they'll not find easily. You quite forgot yours, dear boy. I found it lying on the ground."

The shame I felt at my own lack of ordinary common sense is not possible to describe. If the Revenue had found the harness, the game would be over. Not daring to look at him, I now turned from the depressing sight of our enemies to a thorough investigation of the room but found little in it to cheer me. Unless we jumped from the window, there was only one exit — the one we had entered by. There was rope in fair quantity but so brittle with age that it snapped apart in my hand. Nails there were, rusting away in a keg — excellent if fired from a cannon, but otherwise quite useless.

Among the dust of centuries I found an old ledger filled with dreary columns of figures, also I discovered a musket without a flint and with the lock jammed.

Then I remembered the pistol and the package that Mr. Wells had given to me.

"I almost forgot," said I, as I handed the package to Matthew. "Your uncle asked me to give you this — though I know what it is; it's food for both of us."

"I would be much obliged if you didn't refer to him as my uncle," he said quietly. "Wells has enough troubles of his own."

He opened the package and divided up the food.

"I'm sorry," he said. "I should have warned you."

"He was most kind to me," I said. "Without him I should certainly be facing the Squire by now." I took a large hunk of meat and bit into it.

For a while Matthew said nothing, only stared at me thoughtfully as he munched his bread and cheese. Then he appeared to make up his mind about something and flicked the crumbs from his jacket.

"You may as well know a little more of our history, since you already know enough to have me hanged twice over," he said. "I wonder if you know anything of a man called Dick Turpin?"

"Of course," said I. "He was a famous highwayman. Everyone knows that."

He nodded. "Quite right. Believe it or not, he was a relative of mine. Old Dick was my grandfather. The family name, you see, is Turpin — not Wells."

80

I was much taken aback by this news and goggled at him in utter amazement. To me he had suddenly become a new and different person altogether.

"Dear boy, you needn't look at me like that," said he with a laugh. "I've not suddenly grown horns. Highwaymen are not much different from ordinary people. They're all bluff and bluster mostly."

"Dick Turpin was a brave man," said I. "Speak for your-self when it comes to bluff and bluster."

"Pshaw! listen to the boy," said he with great scorn. "They never forget a rascal — so long as he looks well on a horse."

"If you're half the man he was," said I with spirit, "you'll be doing well."

"Why, he swung at Tyburn," said he. "Brave or not, he finished at the end of a rope."

"And so he did," said I, "and that's a fact you might spare some thoughts on. However, I understand now about your Uncle Wells. Turpin would be a hard name to bear."

"Aye, they're a narrow-minded lot in small places," said he. "The name Wells sits a lot easier on a landlord than Turpin — and he has a wife and child to keep. Oh yes, there was a great changing of names in our family after old Dick was hanged. But you know, he was neither so bad nor so bold as legend made out. He was a man of spirit. The times were out of joint for the likes of him."

I peered through a crack in the shutters. "Times haven't changed much," said I. "Not judging by the soldiers and bloodhounds I can see quite clearly. There's the Squire him-self, plain as day."

"It was bound to come," said he. "I think they'll break in by the windows. The place is a sieve."

I now considered the terrible danger we were in. The men would enter and take us, dead or alive. It was all up with Stephen Carruthers and the reckless highwayman called Turpin.

Born for hanging! The Squire would hang a Turpin with great relish and make a fine bold reputation into the bargain — perhaps even gain notice from the King. As for me, poor fool, all I would ever stand to gain was a prison cell and iron shackles. Get to Plymouth? I would sooner gain Heaven than satisfy such a humble, simple ambition. At that moment my hatred for the wretched Mr. Blunt knew no bounds.

Sounds from the room below were now distinct. Among them we heard the scraping of a door and the squeak of hinges. Again I peered through the crack in the shutter, noting how the Squire was no longer in evidence and how the others stared at the mill while their horses drank from the stream. The dogs were quite scattered to their own devices. Only a few could be seen, some snuffling at rabbit holes, while others investigated the horses — Matthew's black mare among them — as they stood patiently beneath a large elm tree. Gloomily I turned back to the room. Matthew had set his ear close to the trapdoor and I did likewise, hearing more clearly a low rumble of conversation coming from the room below. There was no difficulty in recognizing the presence of Squire Jenkyns, his ponderous tones were not to be mistaken. He was obviously in the company of Major Baxter.

"I knew the boy was a rascal the moment I set eyes on him. I'll not forgive Wells for this. A fool of a man if ever I met one."

"Sir, I'm suspicious of him, I'll admit," replied the Major. "As for the boy, I don't know. There's more behind this affair than meets the eye. But Wells is no fool, if I may be so bold. He's deep, but he's not a fool."

The Squire gave a snort of disgust.

"If the hunchback is deep, as you put it, then he's a rogue. Honest men aren't deep, Major, not secretive. Wells is secretive. I don't like it."

"That's as it may be," said Baxter. "I'd just like to lay my hands on Turpin, that's all. Because of him the whole district is uneasy. Turpin — I never thought the world would ever hear that name again."

"Blood will out, Baxter," said the Squire, and I could almost see him close his eyes as he said the words.

"I'll have notices printed," said Baxter. "We have a good description of the boy. Wish I could say the same for the highwayman. We might offer a reward, say fifty guineas."

"A nice round sum," said the Squire with satisfaction. "The parish will bear the cost — and be glad to pay it out. Wait, I'll go you one better! Add another fifty guineas if they take the highwayman and another fifty if they take the boy, dead as doornails both — and I'll stand behind the balance. What do you say to that, Baxter?"

"Very handsome of you, sir," said Baxter. "But it's blood money. I'd hate to see the boy shot without a fair trial. Blood money is not to my liking in such cases. There's many a poor man would betray his own father for less. Now, sir, if you don't mind, I'll have that trapdoor open."

Ah, you'll not do that easily, I thought — not with the ladder safe and snug in the attic! But I reckoned without the aid of an old barrel and a box discovered by the Major in some odd corner of the place. Soon we heard a heavy dragging sound, accompanied by much grunting and puffing, coming chiefly from the Squire. Then came more grunting as the Major clambered up this tottering hill and I prayed earnestly for the whole contraption to collapse, preferably on the Squire's head. I discovered that prayers of this kind, however justified, are not always answered, for Baxter managed to attack the trapdoor with alarming firmness and energy. He pushed and even beat upon it with a heavy beam, all the while Matthew and I stood separated from him by barely two inches of stout oak. As we stood there, holding fast to the shuddering ladder, I could feel each powerful blow stinging the very soles of my feet. The next blow, I thought fearfully, will shatter the door to splinters. Mercifully, the thick old wood held together and presently the blows ceased.

"Well, it's jammed for some reason," grunted the Major. "I'll get a carpenter to it, someone with a ladder and tools. I never encountered a more firmly placed door. They knew how to build in those days, I'll say that."

"No one's up there, that's clear enough," said the Squire. "They couldn't get up there without a ladder, anyway, not without wings. I can't understand it, you know. The dogs had a scent, I'd swear."

"Rabbits most likely," snorted the Major. Then I heard

84

him scramble down to the floor and the two of them walk away, their grumbling voices fading into the distance.

For a long time we stood without moving or talking, listening to the far-off noise of men as they searched about the mill. Presently all was quiet again and the hunt moved on across the fields. Matthew took a drink from his water bottle and then handed it to me.

"How does it feel to be worth more dead than alive?" he said. "Fifty miserable guineas alive but one hundred golden, jingling guineas if you're stone cold. How's that for fame, dear boy?"

"I don't think much of it at all, thank you," I said with a shudder. "In any case, I'll sell my life dearer than that, as the Squire might discover. The price of my life might well be his own. I'm no fox to hunt into a ditch."

We had been so taken up with our own anxieties that small heed was given to a gradual failing of the light until, barely able to see a hand before my face, I was driven to the window. Peering forth I saw a world much changed, a somber, sunless world of heavy gray cloud. Even as I gazed, a brilliant flash of lightning and a great smash of thunder made the old ruin shake and tremble. Then the rain came pattering down in scattered heavy drops, increasing in such great quantity that a deluge of water drummed on the roof, cascading down the broken gutters and blotting out all view of the countryside beyond a dozen yards. The hunt had been gone for upwards of half an hour so that we had little fear that our enemies would seek shelter at the mill. On the other hand, as I pointed out to Matthew, the bad weather was an opportunity not easily ignored, since we might escape under cover of it.

"There's sense in what you say," he said, opening the trapdoor. "As for me, I would sooner be dry than soaking wet. Depend upon it, we're safe enough here until nightfall. The Squire will likely bolt for his mansion and a warm fire, with servants bringing him mulled ale and slices of hot roast beef. I know his kind."

The very mention of a warm fire and hot roast beef made my head swim and I did not in the least blame the Squire for taking advantage of his good fortune. For a brief moment I had a vision of the past when I too had enjoyed such comforts. I saw the warm glow of home fires, of loving, happy faces, the sound of laughter and good fellowship. Oh, how distant and far away it all was! And when I remembered Christmas and birthdays, I tell you my throat ached with misery.

"Well, don't stand there gawking," grumbled Matthew, bringing me back to my senses. "Help me down with the ladder. At least we can escape from this bats' belfry."

"Why not leave it here?" said I. "Major Baxter has kindly left his barrel. If they return and find a ladder where none was before — "

"Splendid fellow! How right you are," he exclaimed.

In short, we both managed to scramble down; the most difficult part came with the closing of the trap above my head, but this I contrived to do, so that all was left seemingly undisturbed and unchanged.

"Except for one thing," said Matthew. "That carpenter,

whoever he is, will surely wonder how easily the trap opens. But he'll likely say little about it, I fancy, and collect his fee with a straight face."

To a rogue, all men are rogues, I thought, but said nothing, only looked gloomily out of a window at the pouring rain, wishing I had never left that far-off place, Nova Scotia, much less my recent home in Scotland.

Not the slightest inkling had I of the awful events that lay in store, nor did it cross my mind that my lot could be much worse; nay, that I would shortly look back upon this part of my adventure as a kind of frolic. The time was close at hand when I would remember the Squire's bloodhounds — dare I admit it — with feelings of affection, that I would came to so low a pitch of despair that my present enemies would appear by contrast as friends, and the old ruin of a mill a haven of luxury and comfort.

It was well on into the afternoon when the storm finally came to an end. We agreed then to leave the mill and make a dash for the coast road. Down the stairs we crept in the half-light. There were eerie sounds of creaking wood, of wind moaning and mice scampering; I paid heed to none of it, thinking only of escape, yearning only to be in a ship miles away at sea. True, I was now a hunted man with a price on my head and this no fault of mine; but once on the road to Plymouth not all the squires and magistrates in England would ever stop me — at least so I thought.

"There is a great gap in the floor where I hid the saddles," said Matthew. "Follow me and tread carefully. If I dared, I'd strike a light."

At the rear of the mill he knelt and started rummaging, with me all eager to help and never, alas, a thought for the open door at our back.

As I leaned over to lift a saddle, I felt the muzzle of a pistol cold at the base of my neck and a voice — very ugly and familiar — bade me offer no resistance lest I be shot.

10

The Fight in the Old Mill

It was Sweeney; next to him stood Mr. Blunt. Each held pistols and the sight of these wretches — especially Blunt — was a great shock to me.

"Saw the black mare," said Sweeney, "poor old Smiley's gray alongside. Recognized 'em on the instant. Never forget a horse. Thought we'd drop in."

"Now you can drop out," I said. "The quicker the better."

"Good-by," said Matthew.

"Come, now," said Sweeney, "that's no way to treat old friends. Went to a lot o' trouble findin' ye, we did. Lucky we saw the mare. ' 'Ello,' I sez, 'they've come to anchor in the mill.' Ain't that true, Mr. Blunt?"

"Too much gab," said Blunt. "A sight too much gab."

"If you stay long enough, you'll likely meet the Squire," said Matthew, "also his bloodhounds, and the Revenue. You won't much care for that."

"Met 'em already!" cried Sweeney. "An' a nicer gent than the Squire I never 'ope to meet." He swaggered triumphantly, looking mighty pleased with himself.

89

" 'We're lookin' for two rascals,' sez the Squire, when The Bosun and I bump into 'em on the road.

" 'Two rascals?' sez I, looking at Blunt. Unnervin', it was.

" 'What do they look like?' sez Blunt (quicker thinker is old Blunt).

" 'Oh, one of 'em is a young lad. 'E may be travelin' alone,' sez one.

" 'On the other 'and he may be in company with a dangerous 'ighwayman,' sez the Squire, 'name of Turpin. Very dangerous, 'e is.'

" 'Was this lad you speak of big for 'is age, brown hair, and talks back like a sea lawyer?' sez I.

" 'That's 'im to a T,' sez the Squire, all excited. 'If you saw 'im, it's your dooty, my good man, to tell us where 'e went.'

" 'No need to tell us our dooty,' sez I again. 'Off to fight Napoleon, we are. As for them rascals, why, sir, we saw 'em both — the 'ighwayman along of this swab of a boy.' Then I points toward Land's End, and the Squire (bless his old 'eart) goes rushin' off up the road — dogs, revenue men and all."

Covertly I looked from one pirate to the other, managing, while Sweeney talked, to draw a little closer to Blunt, gaining not more than a foot perhaps, but nonetheless a valuable distance if an opportunity should present itself for attack. Something in Matthew's expression told me he would risk a sudden move, pistols or not. As I have said before, he was reckless beyond all meaning of the word.

"If ye don't mind," snapped Blunt, "I'd just as soon get down to business."

"I'd like to be about my own business, if it comes to that," said Matthew stiffly. "But I won't forget this. You took us unawares or you'd be flat on your backs and not likely to get up again."

"You're the one ain't likely to get up if ye don't 'and over the diamonds," growled Blunt. "A ball right between the eyes, that's what you'll get. 'And over the stuff, and no more gab."

Silence followed. Not another word was said while we gazed at each other like wild animals ready to fight.

"Diamonds?" said Matthew presently, in tones of utter bewilderment. "What in Heaven's name are you talking about?"

The change that came over Blunt when he heard these words was terrible to see. First he grew red, then the color all seemed to drain away and I noticed a twitching nerve about his lip. I think he sensed, as I did, a genuine innocence in Matthew's denial, and this he could not bear.

"'And over the necklace," he whispered, with a horrible intensity. "'And it over, I say, or I shoot ye where ye stand."

"I give you only my solemn word," said Matthew steadily, "I do not have this diamond necklace you speak of." He turned to me. "Do you, Mr. Carruthers? — or are we both mad?"

"I haven't the slightest idea of what Mr. Blunt is talking about," said I. "Not the slightest. Nor do I care."

There was a moment's terrible silence. Then Sweeney spoke in low nervous tones.

"Try to keep cool, Mr. Blunt. Nothin' gained by lost

temper. Please cough up them diamonds, Mr. Turpin. Pray be sensible before matters go too far."

"Shut up!" cried Blunt, almost foaming at the mouth. "Take off them jackets, both of ye. Throw 'em on the floor — and quick about it."

This we did. Sweeney went through the pockets, under The Bosun's watchful eye, without result, of course. The riding saddles were closely examined; all the while Blunt's voice grew higher and more strident. He was desperate with rage. Inevitably the search came to a dead end.

"Are you satisfied, Mr. Blunt?" said I. "It strikes me you go to a lot of trouble for nothing"

"For nothin', ye say!" he cried, his face purple. "No, boy, it's no trouble. I've nursed them diamonds from France to

Scotland and from Scotland to Wales, to Devonshire, with murder doggin' me, every step of the way. A king's ransom, that's what them baubles are worth." He breathed so noisily, his face worked so horribly that I feared he might fall down with a seizure then and there. He stuck his face close to mine and I felt the cold muzzle of the pistol on my chest.

"Oh, no, it weren't no trouble, boy. If I've lost the French necklace — from the crown jewels, it is — why then I've lost my last chance to live easy in this world, that's all. My last chance to be rich, d'yer hear?"

Then he gave me a sharp poke with the pistol and fairly spat at me.

"You young swab. You were in the brig, pryin' and sneakin'. Found out about 'em, didn't yer — though how ye did it fair beats me."

"It's a lie!" I said desperately.

"Then you and this swab of a 'ighwayman — oh, it's all clear as rum 'n' water. Ye've diddled me, so yer have, and done yerselves in too, for all the good yer sneakin' and thievin' is likely to get ye."

The smart click of the hammer on his pistol sounded like a death knell.

"Wait," said Matthew. "I believe I know where your treasure is, Mr. Blunt."

The Bosun swung away from me toward Matthew. As he did so, I grappled with him. At the same time Matthew dealt Sweeney such a terrible blow with his fist that Sweeney dropped to the floor like a stone. The Bosun fired off both pistols — the first by accident, since I had him by the wrist

93

and his finger pressed the trigger — the second by intent, the ball coming so close that it fanned my cheek. With all this noise of exploding powder my head sang like a beehive.

"Well done, Steve," grunted Matthew. "Tie up Sweeney. I'll take care of Blunt."

Using their own kerchiefs we soon had both men under our control, their hands tied securely behind their backs. Thus in a twinkling our fortunes were completely reversed. We had their pistols, their powder and ball, and also (looking at Mr. Blunt lying at my feet) their undying hatred.

"Ye'll pay dearly for this, both of ye," gasped The Bosun. "I'll get even, if it takes the rest of me life."

Hurriedly we put on our jackets. Sweeney groaned and struggled to sit up.

"We haven't finished our conversation," said Matthew. "As I said, I do believe I know where your treasure is. Call it a strong suspicion."

"If I 'as to hunt ye over the entire world, I'll have yer 'eart for this," growled Blunt. "I'll cut ye down like pork. If I 'as to walk to Africa and back I'll have yer neck between my 'ands."

"Squire Jenkyns had ample opportunity to take any valuables that may have been in the coach," continued Matthew, ignoring The Bosun. "In that case, why blame us?"

"I'll tell ye why!" cried The Bosun. "Because the Squire ain't got no valuables from no coach — because we were searched by the Squire's men, as rude as ye please, they were. 'What d'ye expect to find on poor, innocent seamen?' sez I.

'Perhaps a diamond necklace,' sez he, 'worth two 'undred thousand pounds!' "

"Aye, and it's rude to treat innocent seamen like that," said Matthew scornfully. "Your stories aren't quite the same, Mr. Blunt. In any case, you and the Squire have things in common, it seems. Well, sir, I leave you to him, and good luck. Come, Steve."

"Wait!" cried Blunt, in tones of great agitation. "Wait and 'ear me out. We can reach an agreement. On a lee shore, I am, on account of you. But ye're smart, ye are; so — fair enough. I daresay I'd take the same advantage meself if I was in yer shoes."

"I daresay indeed," murmured Turpin. "What are you trying to tell me, sir?"

"Only this," said Blunt, and the words seemed wrung from him. "Only this. We can share and share alike; a sort of partnership, ye might say, like me and Sweeney 'ere."

"Enemies we was, at one time," said Sweeney.

"Shut up!" growled Blunt. "Let me do the talkin'. We formed a partnership, like I said, and came to an agreement."

"For your mutual benefit," remarked Matthew.

"Exactly; how well ye put it!" said Blunt admiringly. "I meet up with Sweeney sudden like, on the road. All ready to fight we are, until 'e tells me that Gimp and Smiley are dead. ' 'Old on,' sez he. 'Dead and under 'atches they are, shot by a swab of a highwayman.' "

"At your service," said Turpin, with a bow, "and that's well put, too." Matthew stared coldly at the two wretches.

95

"Ye'll never be able to sell it, not for its proper value," moaned Blunt. "Ye'll let it go to waste, for a song, most likely. There's higher-ups in government as wants it bad — and they're willing to pay." He wrung his hands in agitation. "Oh, they'll pay, a king's ransom and more besides." His voice sank to a whisper and his lips began to twitch. He looked at us, in the half-light of that gloomy place, and on his face was a horrible pleading look.

"I have not got your necklace," said Matthew, crisply and firmly. "I won't say I'd not take it if I had the chance. But the plain fact is, sir, that at this very moment I do not have your necklace. But" — and he twirled his revolver again — "I promise you, sir, that I shall keep an eye out for it. If I should ever come across it, at any time, I will let you know."

"I'll not forget this day's work," whispered Blunt. "I'll have revenge for it, too, and satisfaction. Be ye lord of a manor, if ye ride in a coach and talk easy to kings and queens, why, you swab, I'll get ye, even as ye sits at table or sleeps in yer own bed."

Matthew looked thoughtful. "Perhaps in that case I should act wise before the event," he said, twirling his pistols. "I've half a mind to put an end to both of you, here and now. You could hardly blame me, Mr. Blunt, under the circumstances."

I felt a sudden new grimness in the air and my heart sickened. I pulled Matthew by the sleeve, inclining my head toward the door.

"There's been enough killing," I said. "Let us be away from here, before the light fails."

11

At the Inn of the Ancient Mariner

Mounted once more on our horses, we jogged along the Plymouth road.

"So, our genteel Squire is interested in French diamonds," said Matthew. "How did he know about 'em, I wonder."

I cared little about the subject of the conversation. The moon was up, bright enough to read by; the road was clear and led away to Plymouth — away from Squire Jenkyns, Mr. Blunt, Sweeney and everything connected with the fateful gems. Even Matthew Turpin I would soon leave behind (or so I thought) to pursue all the diamonds in the world for all I cared. As for me, I looked forward to nothing better than a ship, any ship, going away in any direction, with me as a member of the crew.

"Soon we must go our several ways," said I. "You have my thanks for dealing with the pirates."

"I'll be more than sorry," he answered. "You've been a rare good partner, I'll say that. I'm not likely to find another that cares so little for money. The profits are all on my side."

"I might have been murdered but for you," I answered.

97

"Nay, there's no doubt about it. I'm under an obligation to you, nor will I forget it in a hurry."

"Stuff and nonsense," he answered impatiently. "Life's a matter of give and take. Let's not count obligations like a banker counts change. You owe me nothing except the favor of your goodwill."

Well, he had that, as I told him. We continued on for almost an hour, discussing our hopes and plans for the future, with me, I am ashamed to say, talking about myself at great length while Matthew listened with solemn patience.

Presently, at his insistence, we turned off the main road, taking a roundabout route nearer the seacoast. Pursuit was always a possibility; the main roads were likely watched and certainly more dangerous. Our way now was utterly lonely and desolate. On my left I heard the distant pounding of the waves on the shore while on my right were dark shadows of trees and the moonlit slopes of low hills. Not a glimmer of man-made light was to be seen. Not a cock crowed or a dog barked.

As the miles went by I became aware of the moon fading, of a growing dimness all about us as fog rose up from the sea. We dismounted finally, unable to see our hands before our faces, to lead the sweating horses, groping our way forward like blind men.

"Fortunately there's an inn close by, the Ancient Mariner," said Matthew. "Not a place noted for its hospitality but they likely have food and a bed. We can't go on like this."

"You can have your inn," I said, vastly irritated. "As for

me, I intend to keep going, fog or no fog." I floundered then into a pothole brimful of water. My horse had more sense than I for he stoppped at the edge and watched me as I clambered to my feet, covered in mud.

"If you have a mind to swim to Plymouth, you're going the right way about it," laughed Matthew. "Such language! I'm surprised and shocked."

"Make the most of it!" I snapped, shivering with cold and seething with bad temper.

I stopped scowling as a thought — an echo from the recent past — suddenly flew into my head.

"The inn you spoke of," I said. "Was it the Ancient Mariner?"

"Aye, the very one," he replied cheerfully. "A rare gloomy place, so I've been told, but you can likely dry your breeches before a fire."

The Ancient Mariner; had I not heard Sweeney mention it when I was captured by the pirates?

" 'It's gettin dark, we'll never make the Mariner at this rate.' " A snatch of conversation between Sweeney and the late Mr. Smiley — it came back to me, clear as a bell.

I told Matthew about the incident, how it came about that I already had acquaintance with the inn — at least by name. He whistled in surprise.

"If that doesn't beat all," he said. "Oh, it's a pirate's nest right enough. In my trade, a reputation gets about. One hears things. We can't risk trouble at this stage of the game, worse luck. And here we are bedraggled and hungry." He gave me a sideways look. "There's only two of us. We'd likely be no match for, say, half a dozen."

"As to that," I said, "we shall see."

The upshot of it was that, after half an hour of walking, we found ourselves outside a dark, gloomy building. A sign bearing the likeness of an old sailor hung from one corner, and from the window a dim light, barely discernible, cast a feeble trace upon the ground beneath. I knocked boldly on the door.

Barely had the echoes died away when the window above our heads flew open and a voice demanded, not what we wanted, but who we were.

"Travelers in search of lodgings," answered Matthew crisply.

"Who sent you?" came the reply, with keen promptness.

"Your inn was highly recommended by the Prince of Wales," said Matthew with great dignity, and much to my surprise.

"Ho, was it now," said the voice, with undisguised suspicion. "Fancy that!"

" — and by Captain Deadlock," continued Matthew, without blinking an eye. "Oh, you're well known, you are, sir, far and wide."

Silence hung in the air, palpable as the fog. No quick answer now from above; instead a tense moment of silence, a muttered, "I'll be down, sir, if you'll wait," and a scraping sound of the window being closed.

"That's done it for sure," whispered Matthew.

"We'll end this night with our throats cut, mark my words,"
I said. I hadn't the slightest doubt of it.

He came to the door, an ugly short man with a cast in one
eye. He held aloft a lantern and by its light examined us.
His gaze, because of the squint, was uncertain in its direction,
full of suspicion and the shiftiness of someone well acquainted with crime. If it be wrong to judge a man by his
appearance — as it surely is — I can only observe that in
this world are signs so clear in their message that even the
blind may catch the meaning. On the face of this man murder was writ large. I promised myself not to sleep that night

in a room without a strong bolt on the door or without a fully loaded pistol close to my hand.

"You did say Deadlock?" he asked again, his eye swiveling at us. "Yes, I thought you did. I can put you up, of course, nothing fancy. You come at an awkward time."

His voice echoed in the empty parlor as we followed him inside. A feeble apology of a fire flickered in the grate, a single candle burned on the mantelshelf. I never saw a place so drear and deserted.

"Call me Seymour," he said. "And what names shall I put in the book?"

"Names are best left out of it," answered Matthew shortly. "You might say we're on secret business."

"Just so," said Seymour, his eyes more uncertain than ever. "Just so. Secret business. Of course."

"You may describe us as merchants from London, looking for goods of a profitable nature," continued Matthew, "beyond that I'd rather not go."

"Of course," said Seymour. "I understand perfectly. I might just be able to put you on to something — the very thing you describe. I have connections in all parts of the world. London merchants, you say? There ain't enough business in these parts to keep a flea alive. I envy you, sir."

"About our horses," said Matthew sternly. "You have stabling here no doubt. We require the best for them, if not for ourselves."

"Of course, sir," said the landlord, his bad eye swivelling madly. "Of course. Where's that boy!" He shouted. "Ben, Ben!" at the same time clapping his hands until a sallow-faced youth appeared from the kitchen region. At his master's bidding, he took charge of our mounts, though Matthew supervised their welfare in the stables while I dried my breeches before the fire. To do the landlord justice, he bustled about, poked up the fire to suit my purpose and served us, generally speaking, better than I first expected.

But underneath it all the magic of the name Deadlock, magic that in a sense had caused my wet clothes to dry and our stomachs to be filled, was the evil influence that made our host civil and this knowledge in no way made us easier in our minds. He tried every way he knew to discover more of our business but Matthew for one sidestepped all his approaches and I played the part of a foolish apprentice without much trouble.

There was such an air of wickedness about that place that I longed (since I was now dry and fed) to be away on the road, whatever the perils. When we had a chance to discuss the matter, Matthew dismissed any danger of pursuit, observing that we had come off the main road and so dense a fog would likely discourage our enemies altogether. Furthermore, as he whispered, he had a notion to leave the inn long before dawn. This I eagerly agreed to and felt vastly relieved at the prospect.

A clock in the parlor conveniently chimed the hours and this we agreed would signal our departure at midnight. These arrangements we hurriedly made while our landlord was absent in the kitchen, though I had the uneasy feeling that he watched us pretty closely through the keyhole.

He showed us to our rooms finally, lodging Matthew at

the far end of the upstairs passage and me near the stairhead. Once inside I shut the door and turned the rusty key. Then I loaded my pistol, placing it close to hand on a small table. Next I examined the window and with considerable effort managed to slip the catch. Leaning out I saw only a misty dark void. I had the impression that I faced the front, that is, the road, and beyond it the sea. There was a gentle creaking sound as the inn sign moved back and forth slightly in a faint breeze, also the distant sound of waves tumbling on the beach. Closing the window, I then lit a modest fire from a few sticks of wood lying in the grate. Soon a flickering glow pervaded the room and with a candle on the mantelshelf I settled down in my chair to await the appointed hour.

12

What Happened at the Inn

I DECIDED to snuff the candle presently and to keep myself awake turned once again to the window which I opened. The slight breeze had, by this time, grown stronger. The inn sign now swung back and forth with a steady grumbling noise. The fog began to disperse, like a ghost fading away and a pale moon struggled through the clouds, low down above a dark sea. There was a faint gleam of light on water.

Ah! I thought, soon I will once again be afloat, wafted toward a new life; away from all those torments and terrors that had been my lot since leaving Glasgow in the coasting brig. No sooner had these pleasant fancies drifted into my head than I heard a sound of horses approaching along the road. With my head half out of the window, I listened intently, my senses alert to possible danger.

A damp, chill breeze struck my face, the wooden sill beneath my hand was fog damp and moisture crept down walls and gutters. A sort of dampness, it seemed, even entered my very heart as the clip-clopping of hoofs came steadily closer, only to stop at last at the inn door beneath.

There came (after a deal of banging on the door) a shaft

of light upon the road as the door opened, and the shadows of men and horses. I heard the low voice of the landlord and the unmistakable voices of Sweeney, Blunt and, of all people, Squire Jenkyns! The manner of their greeting was not the manner of strangers but of persons well known to each other; of men familiar, not only with our squinty landlord but, I could guess easily enough, with others like him; members of a dark crew, pirates and robbers every one.

The relentless logic of events! In a flash I realized how foolish we had been to seek shelter at the Ancient Mariner, a place known to Matthew as a haunt of pirates. Once set free (no doubt by Jenkyns) where else in all the world would these men come if not to the door of this very inn?

Cursing our bad luck and worse judgment, I retreated into the dark room and considered a moment what best to do. Matthew must be warned immediately. Even as I moved toward the door, guided by a faint glow from the coals still flickering low in the grate, I heard his discreet knock. He stood there, holding a candle. One glance at his grim face was enough; our visitors had not arrived without his knowing.

"Lock your door and pocket the key," he whispered. "We may yet escape this trap."

I had need of only one thing from the room: my pistol. Then I locked the door (as quietly and easily as I could) and followed him along the hall to the back stairs.

His strategy was obvious and simple: while they were at the front we would escape by the back. Unfortunately this simple plan was made complicated by our enemies' presence in the kitchen rather than the parlor, so that we crouched halfway down the stairs, not daring to move, fearful of every breath we took, listening to their talk as they conversed together not above a dozen feet away.

"Well, it's a bit of luck; devil looks after 'is own sometimes" — came the harsh voice of Blunt — "ain't no mistake according to your description, Seymour. Can't be another pair like 'em within a hundred miles. It's death to the both of 'em, I say, before morning."

"We are not here for vulgar revenge, Mr. Blunt," answered the Squire. "Diamonds are what we're after, not blood. You people are all the same; no common sense at all. It's a fair wonder to me you haven't been hanged long ago. Keep your mind on the main business at hand."

"None of that preacher stuff," returned Blunt angrily. "I'll not stand for it. You ain't sitting on your magistrate's throne now, Mr. Squire."

"Voices down, gentlemen," said Sweeney. "We don't want to alarm the birds. Control your temper, Mr. Blunt. T'ain't polite to argue with the Squire. Mr. Seymour, you might stoke up the fire a trifle since there ain't one in the parlor. It's the cold makes The Bosun short in his temper, I shouldn't wonder."

"For one thing," continued the Squire, "how do you know the highwayman has the diamonds? You searched Turpin, you searched the boy. Did a thorough job, according to you. I searched the boy myself, for that matter."

"That I did, right enough. But if Turpin ain't got 'em, then it leaves only yourself," growled Blunt. "Take yer choice."

I could almost feel the Squire draw himself up to his full height and look down his nose at The Bosun.

"That will do, Mr. Blunt, if you please. I'm not here to be insulted."

"True enough," said Blunt. "Ye're here because of money, that's what, same as me. No jewels, no money, sez you."

"I'm only an agent, Mr. Blunt, acting for persons highly placed in governing circles. Once the royal gems are in my possession you will be paid. You know the arrangements."

"Aye, well enough; and profitable are these arrangements to you, Mr. Squire," said Blunt.

"I take risks, grave risks," returned the Squire.

"Risk? Why sir, ye don't know the meanin' of the word. The risks I took to lay my hands on them jewels! Now all for nothin', because of those swabs upstairs."

"We shall soon know the truth of it, Mr. Blunt. I'm just as eager to get at the bottom of this as you are. We all have pistols. If Mr. Seymour can supply us with a sword or two I believe we may deal with these rascals more easily. Mr. Turpin, at least, is highly dangerous and the boy is no weakling."

"Very wisely observed," said Sweeney. "Take 'em as they sleeps, with cold steel at their throats."

"I always keep a sword and a dagger behind the bar," said the landlord. "Also a pistol, fully loaded. One never knows, in this business."

"Very wisely observed, I say again," said Sweeney. "You can't trust a soul."

"Produce these weapons as quickly as you can, Mr. Seymour," said the Squire. "Let us not waste time."

"And what happens if they don't cough up the jewels?" said Blunt. "What if they don't have 'em, like ye say?"

"I never said so, Mr. Blunt," returned Jenkyns sharply. "But if we don't recover this valuable treasure from their persons, why then we shoot the pair out of hand. In fact, we shoot 'em anyway. They know far too much about this affair, far too much."

At least, as I told myself, we knew where we stood with Squire Jenkyns. Then he inquired after a frigate, whether "she had shown herself," as he put it, because he had certain dispatches and letters "for the other side."

"We'll hear from her at any moment, according to news I received only this very day," replied Seymour.

"Good," answered the Squire. "That settles it. We can't have those two spying about and free to come and go. They must be dealt with immediately."

To our vast relief the company then retreated to the parlor. Quickly we made our way down the stair and out by the back door. The air was clearer now. Across the cobblestone yard we saw a light from the open stable door and the moving shadow of the boy called Ben as he tended the horses. We also observed, to our dismay, the burly figures of two men, sentries no doubt, ordered to keep a watch.

"Pirates or Revenue — who are they?" whispered Matthew. "Not that it makes any difference. Curse them! We can't get the horses!"

"Any moment now and they'll discover we've gone," said I. "Then the hunt will be on, and no mistake."

Even as I spoke a window flew up.

"Ho there below," — I recognized Seymour's voice — "keep a sharp lookout. The birds have flown!"

"The 'orses are still 'ere, Squint," shouted a guard.

"Shut 'em up, then," cried Seymour. "Ben'll give you the key. Then scatter about and find them two; they can't be far. Shoot on sight, no questions asked." He bobbed his head in; then, almost at once, bobbed it out again.

"Squire says there's a reward," he shouted. "Jump to it, lads!"

There was a deal of commotion from the inn, with much running to and fro. Blunt's voice could be heard cursing and swearing, answered by the complaining whine of Sweeney. Perhaps less than half a minute yet remained to us, while the guards locked the stable and the rest of them argued the situation.

"The beach!" I whispered· "We can hide among the rocks. They'll search the road up and down, and there's not enough cover in the country behind us for a mouse to hide. The beach is our only chance."

"You're right," answered Matthew. "Across the road then, and hope we're not seen. But first, over the wall."

A low stone wall enclosed the innyard. This we climbed, the rough flints skinning my hands. On the other side was coarse field grass. Bending low, we ran beside the wall until it terminated near the road. Peering cautiously around, we detected no sign of a guard.

"Now," whispered Matthew, "we must make a rush for it. Are you ready?"

"Yes," said I, drawing my pistol. "I am ready."

13

I Become a Smuggler

WE SCUTTLED across the road, tumbling and sliding down the steep bank on the far side. For a moment I lay perfectly still. My face was in the sand, my outstretched hands clutched the tough grass that grew there in clumps and tussocks. My sudden weight disturbed a quantity of sand that ran away in a small avalanche to the beach a good fifteen feet below. At any moment now, I thought, we shall be discovered and shot, or dashed to pieces on the rocks below, and that will be the end of us.

Presently I looked about, spitting sand from my mouth. Realizing the loss of my pistol, I muttered under my breath, determined to recover it; no doubt it lay somewhere on the beach.

As best I could, I slid and scrambled the rest of the way down and tumbled at last, not on rocks, but on a bed of smooth damp sand. Here I was lucky enough to find both my pistol and Matthew Turpin, who was sitting on a rock groaning and holding his head. He, poor fellow, had fallen to the very bottom in one swoop. But he soon recovered, so that we came out of the affair with no worse damage than a shaking up and a few bruises.

We came presently to look about us, and the darkness of that place, the solitude and eerie whisper of the sea, all conspired to lay a sort of spell on us. We have fallen into the next world, I thought, dead men walking in the land of spirits, having been shot by Jenkyns or killed falling down the cliff. I even pinched myself to see if perchance I was dead and turned into a ghost. Fog rolled in from the sea, making the air misty and the shape of things uncertain. A shadow might be a rock — or then again, a crouching man. I imagined a faint clanking sound, as of chains, and the murmur of distant voices — or was it the sea whispering among the beach stones at the tide's edge?

Once I was startled to see a faint light suddenly appear, then as suddenly vanish, as if someone had lit a candle only to have the night breeze snuff it out. This world, I thought, is not clear enough by half. As we crept cautiously forward beneath the cliff, I considered that the darkness might well be a cloak for unspeakable dangers, hiding mysteries of a most unpleasant kind. Indeed I almost wished myself back at the inn, taking my chances with the pirates. But the murderous intentions of the Squire came to mind and I realized that whatever lay before us, there was surely no going back. In short, we could expect only death from the devils we knew, and I for one would rather take a chance with the unknown.

Matthew held his peace, only plodding ahead, looking

carefully at where he stepped. I made him pause for a moment and we stood there listening. He, too, was uneasy in his mind and when we continued on, he stopped again suddenly and gripped my arm.

"This is a strange night and a strange place," he whispered, "and I have no liking for it."

Then, like a sudden crack of thunder, the sound of a distant gun rumbled and echoed across the sea. We stood stock-still, our nerves all on edge.

"The Squire's frigate has arrived, if I'm not mistaken," I whispered, teeth chattering from cold. "Nor is the ship unknown to me, I fancy."

But all speculation regarding the ship was driven from my head in the next minute. To our astonishment first one light, then another — and yet another, appeared until all the beach was alive with dancing lanterns. All was now clear to us, in more ways than one. We had wandered among a gang of smugglers.

We stood dangerously close to five big wagons, each one loaded with boxes and barrels. We saw the shadowy forms of men as they struggled with the cargo, lifting heavy burdens down upon the shingle. A lantern began moving back and forth — without the slightest doubt a signal directed toward the frigate. I looked out to sea; sure enough a light bobbed up and down in answer.

The scene was, in its way, strange. The flickering lanterns, the dim shapes of men and horses, all had suddenly sprung up, it seemed, from the very stones of the beach, as if they had come in some magic way. But the frigate was real enough, along with her cannon, though I daresay there is something magical about contraband when you consider the quick and silent way it comes and goes. This was smugglers' business. It reeked of gunpowder, it reeked of treason, and for the Squire, it reeked of money — and there is a deal of magic in *that* for men like him.

A torch was soon lit and stuck upright in the sand, thus we stood revealed to any who cared to look our way — and look our way someone did, before we had a chance to hide or scuttle off.

"Come on, George," cried the rough voice of a smuggler, " — you too, Bert; don't just stand there; give us a hand, we ain't got all night."

"Well, it's a dark world," I said quietly, my heart sinking.

"And a rummy one, too, by the sound of it," said Matthew. "You be George and I'll be Bert." We moved off toward the wagon.

"We can only try our luck," he said, "and hope for the best."

So, in a twinkling, I was changed into a smuggler and found myself, strange though it was, helping to shoulder heavy boxes that doubtless contained valuable merchandise, though to what port or country it was destined I had yet to find out.

Our situation was now both desperate and easier; desperate because if the smugglers should discover our deception they would undoubtedly kill us; and easier because we were now lost in the crowd. The uncertain light was our salvation, also their need for our labor. Our clothes were torn, our faces no doubt were extremely dirty; to that extent we looked very like smugglers. And since we worked with a will (indeed, our lives depended on it) and at a task all were anxious to finish, no man questioned us. Moreover, it soon became obvious to me that our smuggler, that is, the one who had first hailed us, was a man who liked rum overmuch, for he staggered and talked thickly to himself as men in drink often do.

I thought surely I lived in a nightmare, that nothing I saw was true and that all would vanish in a twinkling. In a daze of unbelief, I shouldered a box and set it down upon the sand, noticing as I did so that a lock had somehow come unfastened. Almost without thinking, I dragged it to the side of the wagon, away from the light. Then I lifted the lid high enough to feel inside and in this way discovered that the box contained bolts of cloth but was only, at best, half-full. Well, I thought, the box has been pilfered and there is no honor among thieves, not even in a nightmare.

Then, to my consternation, as I heaved another box, I saw Jenkyns, Sweeney, Seymour and the rest come trotting up on horseback in our direction. Setting the box down I glanced about wildly for Matthew. He was nowhere to be seen. I looked again toward Jenkyns and the pirates and saw the Squire talking to a smuggler, the one who, I was pretty sure, had first signaled the frigate. The Squire was so close to me that I clearly perceived the silver buttons on his bulging waistcoat. Only one glance in my direction and he must surely recognize me! Crouching low, my heart beating wildly, I scurried around the cart to the half-empty chest. Without more than a last brief glance around for Matthew, I opened the lid and crept inside. As I let the cover down over me, I prayed that my dark haven would not become a coffin through the effects of suffocation; that enough air might leak in to permit me to breathe.

For the time being at least I was safe from detection, though I worried greatly about Matthew and where he might be. Lying there I listened for a time to the muffled sounds of men talking and crunching past outside, fearful always that someone would open the box, or worse still, nail it up, or in some way make it impossible for me ever to escape and thus doom me to a wretched and humiliating end.

Presently, what with the utter blackness of the chest and the effects of my recent strenuous exertions, I felt my eyes grow heavy and I soon fell fast asleep.

14

Death of a Pirate

SOME TIME LATER (how long I do not know) I was suddenly awakened by a movement of the box as if someone wrenched at it. The next moment I overheard such a conversation as to put me in a sweat of fear.

"The lock's gone," said one. "Rope it up, I say. No use spilling cargo."

"Let's have a look inside first," said the other. "No use wasting cargo neither, when it comes to that."

Up went the lid before I had time to consider what to do, so I lay among the bolts of cloth, quite paralyzed with fright. Hands felt among the cloth, even fingered the stuff of my jacket, but thought so little, it seemed, of the quality, that the lid was slammed down without further bother.

"Nothing but cloth," said a voice. "Poor stuff, too, judging by the feel. Rope the box up and let's have done with it."

To my unspeakable horror, they began then to secure the box in a most thorough and seamanlike fashion. Limp with terror, I was banged and jostled about like a sack of corn. I struck my head against the lid and bit my tongue as a consequence, barely conscious of the pain as I realized that I was now buried alive unless I revealed my presence to the smugglers. Indeed, I managed to utter one strangled cry.

"Did I bang it down on your foot, Bill?" said one.

"You'd better not," said the other, "or I'll bang you. Up she goes. There, another turn should do it."

"Well, it's a funny thing, Bill, but I coulda sworn you cried out, sort of," said the other. The box was wrenched around so that my head swam.

"Someone's going to cry when they find all that rotten cloth," said Bill. "Sovereigns is what I would have liked, by the powers! Away with it now, to the boat."

Without further ado, and with much swearing at the heaviness of the load, the box was then carried to the water's edge and finally placed, as I could only imagine, in a ship's boat. My ears told me much of what went on, of where I was and what bustle and activity took place all around me. I heard splashing of water as men waded out with other cargo; also I felt the swaying motion of the boat itself. Then, after a while, I heard the order given to cast off and felt the boat move forward as the crew bent to the oars.

Thus, in a most humiliating fashion, I as part of the cargo — and for that matter contraband cargo — was eventually transferred from the boat to the ship itself, to the deep hold of a pirate frigate. Little need be said of how I was tossed and banged about by the crew when the box was hauled over the side and then dumped, without ceremony, into the hold.

But finally I came to rest, the box was no longer manhandled and I was left alone to contemplate with horror my strange predicament — inside a tightly roped box, with no means of escape, and even if I did escape would find myself among a gang of cutthroats who would surely kill me.

Imagine, if you can, the utter blackness of my small prison, matched only by the blackness of my feeling of despair. I heard the last of the other boxes (one at least was piled on top of mine) placed in the hold. Imagine, I say, the retreating footsteps, the voices of the pirates becoming fainter and fainter as they went up to the deck and began the serious business of working the ship. There I was, quite alone, left to die like a rat in a trap.

I did not give up the struggle without testing the timbers of the wretched chest. If I had had a crowbar or an ax I might have hacked my way out. I even prayed to Heaven most fervently, and having reached the lowest fathom of despair, I at last composed my thoughts enough to ask forgiveness for my sins.

We had been at sea for no more than an hour and I had given up all hope of escape when someone began dragging at the box above me. Well, I thought, I would rather die in the open air with the wind on my face than perish alone in darkness and humiliation.

"Help, help!" I cried in a loud voice, receiving in return a curt order to keep quiet hissed at me through the keyhole. Within half a minute the rope was cut and the lid raised. There came a blessed flood of cool damp air. Staring down at me by the light of a candle was the cheerful face of Matthew Turpin.

"Anyone at home?" he inquired. "An odd way to travel, Stevie boy."

Clambering out, I glared at him and closed the lid.

"It was no choice of mine," I said. "How you knew I was in there, I don't know, but I'm much obliged to you."

"I saw you climb in when Jenkyns rode up," said he. "Saw them rope the box. Come on, there's a safe spot behind some barrels at the stern."

Without another word we set the box in its original position and crept around to the rear of the hold.

"Safe for the time being," he said.

"I lead a life of touch and go," I said grimly. "Where is the ship heading for?"

"Well it isn't heading for Plymouth," he said. "I heard talk of Saint-Malo."

"Out of the frying pan into the fire," I said, brushing sweat from my forehead with my coat sleeve. "Why you're roaming the ship like this, free as air, beats me."

"No one knows me, dear boy," he said, setting the candle in front of us, on the floor. The vessel rolled to a gentle, steady swell, and regular creaking sounds came from the cargo as the barrels nudged each other in the gloom.

"Half the men were drunk on rum," he continued. "They had three boats to load up, so there was I, bold as you please, helping, and no one the wiser — or caring — just as long as the job got done. Even old Jenkyns gave me a nod. Can you believe it?"

"You took a dreadful risk," I exclaimed.

"Not at all," said he. "I stuffed my hat in my pocket and they took me for one of themselves in the dark. As for pulling an oar, I can do it quite as well as any drunken pirate. When I helped stow cargo, I simply stayed down here."

"They'll never hang you now," said I. "You're far too lucky to hang."

"Well, it's a short life and a happy one," said he cheerfully.

"Once again I'm in your debt," said I, "nor will I forget it in a hurry."

Then he told me what I had already guessed; that we sailed in *The Good Friends*. This news, though it came as no surprise, made my heart sink. It was certain now that Captain Deadlock steered my destiny and this fact was hard to bear.

"Deadlock is a blockade runner," he said, locking his hands about his knees. "There's a good profit in it, and he's no fool."

"Smart as paint he'll look, hanging from a yardarm," said I.

Matthew gave me a sideways glance. "They'll have to hang a lot of his friends first," said he. "He's a useful man in certain quarters." He pointed to the barrel standing behind us.

"Every pound of cargo you see here is destined for Napoleon's troops," said he. "Jenkyns, Deadlock and Company share the profits. A blind man could see what's going on. Mind you, there's more to it than that. War isn't just a matter

of killing. There's things they call politics and secret trea-
ties."

"It's treason, pure and simple!" cried I.

"Not so loud, dear boy," he whispered, "or they'll hear
you on the quarterdeck."

"I'll set fire to the cargo," I said, "rather than see it fall into
enemy hands!"

"A loyal sentiment very nicely put," he returned, "but
consider your future as a lump of charcoal, Stevie, compared
to your future as a lively fellow able to climb in and out of
boxes at will. As for my future, why, bless your heart, I'll
not even mention it."

I almost called him a coward then but when I thought
of all the terrible risks he had taken to save my life I said nothing and looked away.

In the dark hold of that treasonous ship, the bitter truth
dawned on me of the real nature of my predicament. In
short, I was now on my way to the enemy camp, the country
of Napoleon Bonaparte, the sworn enemy of England. Filled
with dismay at the wicked twist of fate that had brought me
to this extremity, I was quite ready to settle matters with Deadlock in any violent manner that might present itself. Give
me powder, I thought, and I'll blow the ship apart; I'll find
ways and means to bore holes below her waterline; give me
fire and I'll make of her a flaming torch. Ah, but if only Jenkyns and his wretched crew as well as Deadlock might frizzle
in the flames! — and those unknown higher-ups whose shadowy hands were just as surely at the wheel of *The Good*

Friends as those of Captain Deadlock, guiding her, an English ship, to France, all for the sake of gold. Ah! I thought, if only I had them aboard now, along with a barrel or two of Captain Campbell's powder in the hold!

"On the other hand," said Matthew quietly, breaking into my dark thoughts, "What you suggest has interesting possibilities. Now that I come to think about it, setting the ship afire is quite a good notion."

"You take the matter calmly, that we sail for France," said I. "For me it's a hard pill to swallow. I only wanted to reach Plymouth when I set out upon this journey."

He shrugged. "We sail to the wars; that is what you wanted, wasn't it? Only we go via Saint-Malo instead of Plymouth. What difference does it make, after all?"

There was logic in what he said, if not much comfort. Gloomily I listened to the water racing past the bulwarks, gurgling and slapping against the sturdy oak timbers.

"If we continue at this rate, we should arrive there in less than two days," I said. "We could set the blaze just before they start unloading."

"And a nice diversion it would make," said Matthew. "In that way we kill two birds with one stone — we destroy the enemy stores and during the excitement of the fire, we escape."

"Only it's easier to set the fire going than for us to escape," I said. "We can only take our chances as they come."

"I'll not swim," he said dourly, "if that's what you mean. I'll not own another coat like this one. Salt water will be the sure ruin of it."

124

It was comical how he worried about a mere coat when his life was at stake. I remarked that he could always buy another coat but never another life.

"There's nothing much new in that observation," he said coldly. "In any case, the coat is made of rare fine Flemish stuff and I'll not have it spoiled."

We argued the matter back and forth until he finally broke down and admitted that he could not swim a stroke, that if he ever fell overboard he would sink like a stone.

"Nay, do not reproach me for this grave weakness," said he, holding up his hand. "I'm a proud man, but ye'll come to understand that no one can be clever at all things. If I were forced to swim or drown, I'd do my best, but a drowning cat would do better. I'm a born landlubber and that's a fact."

This weakness, as he called it, gave me a pang of concern since we might well find ourselves in no position to choose our method of leaving the ship. For the present we had no way of telling how fate would arrange matters, though I prayed that *The Good Friends* would lay herself conveniently alongside a dock.

In one matter we were lucky: they stored their biscuit and water in the hold so that we ate our fill, albeit the food was dull stuff.

In the early hours of the following day, I decided to investigate the stern of the ship, where I thought the weapons might be kept. Also I had a notion to get a little fresh air after our confinement in the musty hold. Thus, with a brief word of caution from Matthew, I made my way toward the officers' quarters, carrying a stub of candle, but snuffed it out quickly when I saw a light near the quarterdeck ladder. Drawing closer I saw it was the cabin where mutineers were confined or, if need be, where persons suffering from the plague were kept in quarantine. This cabin Matthew had previously described as a possible hiding place and useful to know about. It lay directly beneath the captain's quarters.

The light came from a window secured with crossbars. Drawing closer, I was amazed to hear a voice, a voice I recognized only too well — the voice of Mr. Blunt!

There I was, lurking hard by the companion leading to the quarterdeck; in front was the door and the window of this place. In the extreme of dread, I crept forward, consumed by a fearful curiosity, conscious always that I might well be discovered there by any passing member of the crew. But, dangerous or not, I had to see what took place beyond. I stationed myself to one side of the little barred window and peered cautiously through.

I saw Mr. Blunt seated at a rough table. On the cabin floor, back against the wall, was Sweeney, looking, I thought, quite ill. Standing with his back to me was Captain Deadlock, a heavy cutlass in his hand.

"All for nothin'. Not a penny gained by it," raved Deadlock. "Botched; scuppered by a mere boy and a rat of a highwayman. I'll see ye rot for it, and Sweeney, too."

"If I had 'em both 'ere now," cried Blunt, clenching his hands, "I'd have 'em by the thumbs. The lash, I'd give 'em, and the rest of it, until they cried for mercy."

"Thought ye'd keep the stuff for yerself," scoffed Deadlock.

"Thought ye'd diddle me, like the pig ye are — " he swung the cutlass, making a hideous whistling sound. "Thought ye'd slip yer cable and break the oath, you swab, with never a thought for yer old messmates. Oh no, not you. Never so much as a nod or a farthing." He swung the cutlass again. Then he stepped forward and leaning across the table, stuck his face close to Blunt's. The cutlass pointed a bare inch from The Bosun's neck. "The swab ain't yet born who cuts me out!" he hissed. "Not yet born, d'ye hear? Sharp tried it, so did Hooker, an' old Starkey, too, you remember. They all tried it — once only. And they was smart, the most of 'em. Well, you ain't that smart, d'yer hear? Squire sez ye know too much. 'Get rid of him,' sez Squire, 'he knows too much.' 'Oh no he don't,' sez I. 'Blunt ain't got brains enough for a flea.'"

"If I had that boy 'ere now," whispered Blunt, his face ashen, "it would be a different story!"

"Only where is he now? — or the highwayman?" cried Deadlock bitterly. "I'll tell ye where they are, d'yer hear? I'll tell ye. Riding in coaches, they are, spending golden guineas — our guineas — on dainty food and wine and that!"

It sounded very well, but knowing in all truth where I was, that is, not a yard away, I shivered at the thought I might be found there, and glanced fearfully around. But the wind had freshened in the last hour and the crew were kept busy aloft.

Turning my gaze once more to the window, I saw something that froze my blood, and it was Sweeney, creeping up

on Deadlock, with a knife in his hand. Watching there in
the shadows, my eyes as big as saucers, I could neither move
nor cry out, but only wait, under a spell of horror, for the
deed to happen.

The ship gave a steeper roll than usual and Deadlock saw,
from the corner of his eye, the gleaming knife. The wicked
sharp blade missed his neck by a fraction and Sweeney fell
across the table. He looked up at Deadlock, eyes staring,
mouth open to scream. Then with a cry of "Die like the
coward you are!" Deadlock ran him through with the cutlass
and he went to his Maker without a sound.

I waited no longer. In a sort of daze I found my way
back down to the lower hold.

"Are you ill?" whispered Matthew. "You look as if you've
seen a ghost."

"In a way I have," I said, and told him what had
transpired in the cabin. When I had done he shook his head.

He said, "Would you believe such treachery!" Then he
looked grim and thoughtful, staring into space. He had lit a
small lantern, a dangerous thing to do, but he could douse
it, he said, at a moment's notice. The light seemed to make
his eyes unnaturally bright and hard — and I was reminded
of the diamond necklace.

"Blood and money mix uncommonly well," he said, presently. "There's a deal of blood now, on the diamonds. Yours
and mine will be added if we don't watch out."

This event made me very restless and uneasy in my mind.
I found a spot under a skylight so that I could watch the last

stars of night fade away, and for some reason I presently felt a certain calmness come over me. But any peace and quiet I enjoyed was short-lived. The North Star was just fading when I heard a cry of "Land ho!" from the lookout.

Returning quickly to the hold, I warned Matthew and we began our desperate preparations to fire the ship.

15

The Fire Ship

Now THAT MATTERS had gone so far and the flames were about to leap, a sudden pang of conscience overcame me so that I had no more wish to destroy the ship than cut off my own hand. Indeed, I felt such a sadness in my heart when I considered what I was about to do, and such a weakness of decision that I dropped the candle and it was snuffed out harmlessly.

Matthew, without a second thought, applied a sulphur match to the rubbish we had found in a locker. Before I could speak a word of protest the deed was done, past all recalling.

The flames leaped up and up from the packing straw, old sailcloth, tallow, and a quantity of whale oil taken from a lamp. At first there was only a little smoke and then the fire burned briskly among the barrels of cargo.

With one horrified look behind, I ran for the ladder, followed closely by Matthew, coming on the upper deck near the forepeak. It was early morning, the sun not yet up. Looking about I saw with dismay that we had come to anchor a good distance away from the dock, in a roadstead crowded with shipping. They either expected to unload by means of small boats or to await a dockside berth later in the day. So, my friend Turpin, I thought, you will have to swim for it after all.

At any moment the fire would manifest itself and time was surely running out for us. Standing as we did above the anchor chains, I looked down and saw a bumboat, that is, a waterman, who sold trinkets and fruit to seamen. Then and there I made up my mind what we might do.

"Ahoy, what have you to sell?" I shouted. "Come closer, if you please."

"He's a Frenchman, dear boy," said Matthew. "Can't understand a blessed word you say. I take it you have wicked designs on his boat."

"We either get his boat or you swim," said I, "and if we waste another minute we're lost. If you can make him understand, then do so, in Heaven's name."

So Matthew spoke to the old fellow in his own language and without hesitation he climbed the chains like a monkey. What the highwayman said I shall never know but the poor man seemed highly pleased and made his way toward the stern. It was then I noticed a wisp of smoke issuing from the cracks around the foreward hatch.

"People are all the same," muttered Turpin. "Promise 'em something for nothing and off they go, like lambs to the slaughter."

"Quickly!" said I, with a glance of despair at the two members of the crew running toward the hatch. "Over the side with you. Come on, follow me."

I have no distinct recollection of those last few moments

on *The Good Friends* or how we managed to tumble helter-skelter into the bumboat. All I remember is the rusty anchor chains, the water dripping from the great links, and how my fingers trembled with anxiety as I fumbled to untie the boatman's line.

Matthew pulled on the oars and the boat drew rapidly away from the side of *The Good Friends*. From the deck above I heard cries of alarm and smoke could be seen, a great billow suddenly enveloping the ship. We may have been only twenty feet away when there came the muffled, ominous sound of an explosion.

"That's a piece of luck," cried Matthew. "Reached some of their powder."

Not daring to speak, I sat huddled in the stern sheets, gazing with horror at the old ship. The sight made me gulp. Flames were now visible, a tall ugly orange tongue of it arising from the region of the forecastle. It licked at the lower foresail and within seconds the mast was a torch of roaring fire. For some reason, they saw fit to get the anchors up, perhaps with a notion of bringing her clear of other shipping. Her bow swung over in a sudden freshening of the east wind and whether they liked it or not, or whether they could help it, she started drifting toward a great concentration of French and Spanish ships.

Never shall I forget the sight: the flames a raging brilliance against the dark, early morning sky; the masts and rigging crackling and tumbling all about; the dark hulls of ships and the frantic movements of men as they tried to escape the flames or salvage their vessels. I could hear the cries of seamen and saw the ocean turned to red. The sky was black with smoke. It was like the end of the world, and I am not ashamed to say that, for a moment, my courage failed me and I hid my face in my hands. Where were the pirates now — Deadlock and Mr. Blunt? Sweeney was at least out of it; if his eyes stared at the flames he saw nothing and felt nothing. Well, God have mercy on us all, I thought, we are all wicked and there's no one fit to cast the first stone.

The highwayman meanwhile had been whistling a tune to help him with the rowing. I looked up to see his face pink from exertion.

"Do not despair, Steve," said he. "At least we have done more damage to the enemy with one match than old Nelson could with a dozen broadsides. It's no use cringing at the sight of war; not once the guns start firing."

"Men are dying and ships burning on our account," said I. "It isn't a matter to be taken lightly."

"You'll get used to it," said he, shaking his head. "There's a deal of war ahead of you yet, if I'm not mistaken. But aren't I a mighty fine hand at the oars?"

We had, due to his efforts, come a considerable distance away from the burning.

"Give me the oars now," said I, moving carefully forward. "It's a long pull back to England."

"To tell you the truth, I haven't the back for rowing," said Turpin. "I have a mind to steal a fishing boat — any tub with a mast and a rag of sail will do. This is slaves' work."

We exchanged places. I took the oars and began a cautious passage toward shore. While he had been talking I had taken note of just such a vessel as he described, an old, ill-kept boat moored beside a deserted, tumbledown jetty. I pointed toward it.

"There's your craft," said I, pulling on the oars with all my strength.

Thus we arrived presently at a remote part of the harbor, the mist of early morning drifting above the quiet water. A sort of bend or indentation in the geography of the place had cut off the view so that we no longer saw *The Good Friends* or any sign of the fire except a drift of smoke in the north. Between us we had rowed some three miles, as near as I could judge; my hands were fair blistered from the unaccustomed work. Coming near to the old boat, I rested on the oars, studying her closely but saw not the slightest sign of life, either on the vessel or on the land beyond.

"We'll need water, if nothing else," I said. "The old fellow has left us all his stock but there's not much in the way of food, except oranges."

"There's a warehouse, if I'm not mistaken," said Matthew. "We should first examine it; who knows what goods it may contain, useful for a voyage! Let us ashore then. But remember, dear boy, the enemy may object."

Well, as to that, not a human appeared, not a dog or a cat. We tied the boat up to the ancient dock, climbed a rickety stair to the cobblestones above, and I found myself, for the first time in my life, on the soil of France. The cobbles, I noticed, with some surprise, were no different from those of Glasgow, and the trees, when I came to look at them, were no less green.

In the shed or warehouse, we found a quantity of flour in bags, a cheese and a flitch of ham hanging from a beam, and a number of small oak kegs full of vinegar. This useless stuff we emptied away, filling each keg with water from a rain barrel that stood near the door.

So far matters had gone well: we had our water and food enough to keep us alive. The boat was at hand, tied to the dock, a blessed means of escape. With luck we could leave under the guise of fishermen going about our lawful task. But alas, all unknown to us, our luck was fast running out.

After stowing our food on the fishing boat we returned to the warehouse for the water kegs. I remember standing looking about the place and it suddenly came to me that here were stored an odd assortment of things — rope, blankets, saddles, bridles, wheels of carriages, nails, leather buckets; also, when I looked more closely, long wooden boxes containing muskets.

"Quartermaster's stores," said Turpin briefly. "We have the honor to steal from Napoleon himself. I have my eye on a saddle. If we had time — "

With a bang the door behind us was suddenly slammed shut. For a moment, in the gloom, I had a wild, hopeless notion that the wind had played a trick, that we had only to push and the door would open. It took only a moment's effort to prove the notion quite wrong. The big door was closed and bolted like that of a fortress!

"I am very much afraid, dear boy," whispered Matthew, "that we are now prisoners of the French army, and of Napoleon."

From outside we heard a bugle sound. Then we heard shouting, as if orders were being given.

"There was a sentry, I suppose," said Matthew gloomily, "and he finally woke up."

"I'm a long way from Plymouth now," I said, with utter misery in my heart.

16

I Am Made a Prisoner

I BEGAN loading and priming my pistol, quite prepared to make a last desperate fight for my life, but Matthew persuaded me against anything so foolhardy. Instead, we hid our weapons on top of a crossbeam, a kind of shelf that ran along the wall some distance above our heads. Standing on tiptoe we slid the pistols out of sight. The gloom was relieved in part by two narrow slits of windows high up near the roof. Given enough time, I was quite certain we could use them as a means of escape, but they were, as I say, high up and difficult to reach. But there was no time left to us, not even time in which to concoct a story in case we should be questioned, though it was likely they would hang us first and question us afterwards if they connected us with the fire on *The Good Friends*.

This, the most dismal part of my story, will gain but little from any detailed account of what followed; indeed, the very memory of it is so painful to me that I can hardly bear to recall it. Sufficient to say, therefore, that the doors were flung open and we were seized by a captain of the French militia and a company of soldiers. We were searched for weapons, shouted at, and then marched off to prison.

In the cold sunshine of early morning, with the dew still on the cobblestones, they marched us through the narrow main street of the town, our hands tied behind our backs. In my ears was the solemn beating of a drum and the jeers of the populace, wretched poor people, it seemed, judging by the haggard look in their faces and the rags that served them for clothes. I remember a few vegetables being hurled at us and the crowd scrambling for them, as if a turnip or two was golden guineas. I was barked at by starved dogs, and humiliated by the taunts of hungry children.

The dreary procession came to an end at the iron gates of a fortress, a vast stone pile destined henceforth to confine me. This grim place was, as I presently discovered, built on a high rocky peninsula overlooking the sea. On three sides turbulent waves beat against the sheer rock on which the castle was built. Heaven help the escaping prisoner if he attempt to swim for he must surely drown in the undertow or be smashed against the rocks. If he attempted the only exit from land, he must needs run a terrible gauntlet of armed soldiers and heavy artillery. Looking up at the gate, I saw three human heads impaled on the iron spikes, grinning down at me. The captain of militia took pains to point out this ghastly sight and, for my benefit, phrased his warning in tolerable clear English, so that I was left in no doubt regarding my future should I be rash enough to attempt an escape.

I glanced over at Matthew and he gave me a slight wink so I knew that warnings, however deadly or terrible, would have no effect on him if opportunity presented itself. But, as the heavy iron gates closed with a loud clang behind us, closed I say with a noise like the solemn tolling of a funeral bell, all hope of escape vanished from my heart. Never again, I thought, will I hear the song of birds or feel the summer sun on my face. As I descended ever deeper into that awful place, the light gradually faded away until when they left me at last, alone in a dungeon, I sat chained to the wall in almost total darkness.

Thus it came about that my journey from Scotland ended in a French prison. Now quite alone in the world, I had none to speak for me, no one to trouble himself about my whereabouts. Who would ask after me or make inquiries — except perhaps old Captain Mullins now waiting in vain to meet me in Plymouth? The rascal Turpin (whom I now, quite unjustly, blamed for all my troubles) was in no better position than myself and would likely suffer the same horrible fate. Unless immediately executed, we might languish for many years, prisoners in a stone fortress in a foreign land, until at last a merciful death would overtake us. I had a vision of myself grown old, with white hair and a long beard, silly in the head from years of cruel usage and solitary confinement, forgetting perhaps even my own name, having conversation only with rats, hearing only the clank of the heavy chains that kept me in bondage.

In this wretched state I languished for a week. High up near the roof of my cell, a small barred opening let through

a glimmer of light. As to the passing hour, I could hear the
church bells in the village cheerfully count the time to my
next meal of dark bread and water. Early in the morning my
chains were unlocked, permitting me to wash in a bucket
and, if I chose, to exercise by running or walking about
my dungeon for half an hour. After this brief taste of liberty I was again chained up like a dog, and left to my own
thoughts.

This was the only time I had contact with another human
being, though my jailer was so far from talkative that he
merely grunted if I so much as spoke a civil word. His rou-
tine never varied. Each morning, about seven of the clock,

a little sliding panel in the door would be pushed aside; two bloodshot eyes would observe me; the door would then be unlocked and a great hairy giant of a man would enter and unlock my leg chains. He would then depart, leaving my rations and the bucket, returning in a short while to chain me up once more, as I say, like a common dog. And lest it be thought foolhardy for a jailer to release a prisoner, even for a moment, another wretch stood by holding a heavy club, observing my every move with such close attention that I had no more chance of escaping than a mouse from a trap.

On the seventh day my jailer appeared as usual. With a noisy rattle of chains, the heavy iron-studded door was unlocked. But this time, to my surprise, he spoke briefly in broken English, saying in effect that I must leave the cell and come with him. He grinned down at me, showing horrible black teeth. Holding me firmly by the arm, he then led me outside, along the narrow passage.

This sudden change in my otherwise dreary life caused the liveliest speculation in my mind. Where was I being taken? Would they set me free, or — as seemed more likely — was I about to be executed? Would I be tortured? My curiosity in all this was almost more than I could bear. But regardless of these natural feelings of agitation, I managed somehow to keep a sharp eye on everything about me. I counted nine doors, each closely barred and chained. Behind one of these, as I sadly thought, Matthew Turpin must surely languish, unless, of course, he was already dead.

But we soon left this part of the castle. Coming to the end of the passage, we turned on our right, ascended eight stone steps to a higher level, then, turning left, walked along yet another passage, this one quite devoid of doors. Two passages led away at intervals of twenty paces, each one sealed off by a tail iron gate. My jailer stopped before each of these, listening intently to the weird and doleful sounds that emanated from the gloom beyond. He cupped his ear, listening with obvious enjoyment to the fearful noise of men in torment. He smiled, and nodded at me, even winked an eye as if to say that all was quite as it should be, that all these sounds of misery that made my hair stand on end were much to his liking and satisfaction.

"Prisoners," he said with relish, "Royalist dogs. Very bad men."

"Is my friend Matthew Turpin among them?" I said, quite on the spur of the moment, for it occurred to me that my jailer might well know something of his fate. He shook his head.

"Only Royalists in there, I tell you," he said. "Your friend next door."

"Next door?" I said, puzzled.

"Of course. Next door to you," he said with the greatest casualness. "Come, we must not keep waiting the Governor."

This sudden news, come upon almost by accident, caused me to think furiously. Turpin actually in a dungeon next to mine! From that moment I began actively to think of escape. One wretched prisoner quite alone would find great difficulty in gaining his freedom, but two people working together might well have a greater chance of success.

But alas, when I stood at last before the man who could, by merely issuing a command, end my earthly days, almost the first words he spoke left me in little doubt that I would never leave that awful place alive.

17

The Last of Mr. Blunt

With my grinning jailer on one side and a fully armed soldier on the other, I presently confronted the governor of the castle, General Picard. His quarters were in a great tower, on the ground floor, grandly ornamented with carved and gilded furniture. A suit of ancient armor stood in one corner of the room while the paneled walls were hung with tapestries and shields. Through a window I glimpsed many soldiers at drill in the courtyard. Every now and then the ground trembled beneath me as a cannon was fired from the ramparts overlooking the sea. Altogether this castle of Saint-Malo was a most strongly fortified position not likely to be taken easily, either by siege or bombardment from warships. General Picard was quick to notice my interest; his black eyes gleamed with malice as he stroked his neat dark beard.

"Do not trouble yourself to count the soldiers, Monsieur Carruthers," he said sarcastically, "nor for that matter the cannon. Your spying days they are over — forever."

"I am not a spy," I returned angrily. "Your charge is an insult."

He faced me across a table littered with books and maps. Sighing, he leaned back in a comfortable leather chair.

"Then pray explain your presence on French soil," he said. "No doubt your story is a good one. I am quite prepared to be entertained. It is understood, of course, that you will tell me everything except the truth. Never mind. From spies, only lies are expected, is it not so?"

"If the truth should kill me," I said, barely controlling my temper, "you shall have the truth."

I then recounted my story, from the time I left Glasgow to the time I landed unwillingly in the hold of *The Good Friends*. I told of my meeting with Blunt, the horrible chase in the coach, the death and burial of the pirates by Turpin, and my capture by Squire Jenkyns. I held nothing back except reference to the diamonds, for this was Turpin's affair not mine. Also I sensed how the wretched stones constituted a real danger for him and I had no wish to add to his perils. As to the firing of the ship, I trod warily, for here was danger also, of a different kind. The fire had caused the enemy great damage. It was an act of war and if they discovered our part in it matters could go very hard with us. Of the death of Sweeney, I said nothing.

In the end I remarked that it was natural that we should seek to save our lives from a burning vessel. Nay, I even appealed to his gallantry by saying that I expected better treatment, even from our enemies, than to be thrown into a dungeon, since after all we were no better than shipwrecked men.

When I had done, he continued to gaze at me, eyes narrowed, hands locked behind his head. Then he relaxed his attitude, and shuffled among his charts as if at a loss for words suitable for the occasion. At last he spoke.

"You know, Monsieur Carruthers, that in my work I hear many tales; but surely yours is the strangest, most unbelievable, my ears have ever heard. Of course you expect me to believe this — this — fantastic account, yes?"

"Begging your pardon, sir," said I, "that is entirely up to you. I am no spy. I am here in your country much against my will. I can only swear to you, sir, that all I have told you is true — every single word."

He nodded gloomily, giving forth with a heavy sigh.

"Oddly enough, I believe you," said he. "You perhaps leave out one or two things, but generally speaking your story has the ring of truth. As for this man you call Mr. Blunt, we shall deal with him in our own way, along with the English Captain Deadlock."

"I have no cause to like these men," said I, "but if you have mercy in your heart, I would ask mercy for Mr. Blunt at least."

He made no answer, merely inviting me to gaze from the window overlooking the courtyard.

I witnessed a most melancholy sight. For some time I had been conscious of a drum beating slowly and mournfully. Now I saw the procession, drummer first, then a pitiful file of men shackled one to another like slaves, perhaps twelve in all. Among them walked The Bosun and Captain Deadlock.

The sight was shocking to me. Wretches they undoubtedly were, but they were also the unhappy dupes of men like

Squire Jenkyns. That worthy was not in chains, or ever likely to be; yet he used these poor, ignorant men in his profitable, treacherous dealings with the enemy.

To cap everything, Mr. Blunt slowly turned his head, fixing me with a stare so horrible that I flinched as if struck. His look was full of bitter hatred, of recognition and of a terrible misery. As he passed by me he lifted his arms slowly, showing the heavy chains about his wrists, continuing to gaze at me with a hatred I could feel to my very marrow. Then, on a sudden, his expression changed and he smiled at me. He even attempted, regardless of his chains, a mock salute, nor will I ever forget this, the last time I saw Mr. Blunt.

The drum grew fainter and fainter in the distance. Filled with dismay I turned from the window.

"Where are they going?" I asked. "What sort of punishment is this?"

Picard shrugged. "They are lucky," he said. "I might have had them shot. Deadlock is a traitor to France. He posed as a friend. Instead, he brings a fire ship into the crowded harbor of Saint-Malo. This, surely, is an act of war, do you not agree? For this they deserve death, no? Instead I sell them to a powerful sheikh of Morocco. They will end their days chained to the galleys of some Arabian pirate. They are pirates, after all. They will soon get used to such work!"

Galley slaves — chained to the oars! Their dreadful fate stung my conscience; my face grew hot with shame.

"General Picard, these men are guilty of no crime against France," said I grimly. "It was I who set the ship afire. They are traitors to my country and deserve to be punished. But it

148

was I and I alone that planned the fire — this act of war, as you call it."

He laughed and patted me on the shoulder.

"Well, well, so that's the way of it, eh?" he said. "Of a certainty you are a brave fellow. You think cleverly to exchange yourself for two of your countrymen. Yes, indeed you are very brave."

"But it's true!" said I, desperately. "I set fire to *The Good Friends*. I did so only to destroy a cargo destined for the armies of Napoleon!"

He looked at me and his expression was far from friendly. Then he took a pinch of snuff.

"And your friend, Monsieur Turpin?" he asked, blowing his nose. "What part did he play in all this?"

"Ask him," said I. "He can speak for himself."

"Already I have done so," he said. "He told me quite a different story. He said that Deadlock gave orders to burn the ship, that you and he were forced to jump overboard to save your lives."

I knew then how useless it was to press the matter further. Turpin had told a simple lie about firing the ship, but as to the evidence, who could ever prove him wrong?

Picard sensed my discomfiture, it seemed, for his manner toward me softened.

"Never mind, boy," he said. "You are young and have much to learn. All rascals get punished sooner or later and it matters little how they die if death they deserve. As for you and Turpin, I have no worries that you go unpunished, whatever your crimes. Here you are and here you stay. You are much too dangerous and brave a fellow to let loose. Why, my dear sir, you are worth six of those scurvy wretches I sell to Morocco! What a disservice to France if I let you go — you might sink every second ship in our navy. What then would Napoleon think of me, eh?"

He became the brisk official once again and spoke rapidly to my jailer in French. Then he turned to me.

"Orders I have given that your chains shall be removed. Also meat you will receive once a day. You may have also a candle and Bible for one hour in the evening. As to your future — " he shrugged, frowning. "To us you are dangerous, Monsieur Carruthers. It is well that you are safely under lock and key."

"For how long?" said I, my heart sinking.

"Who knows?" said he. "Five years, ten years — how long will this war go on? Perhaps you will be forgotten. In two months I am due to be relieved. My successor is famous for being a harsh man. Me, I am too soft. Because you are young, I leave off the chains; little comforts, like meat, a candle and a Bible I give to you — all because you are young and I am sentimental. The new governor will be more ruthless. He will, I think, shoot you. I hope not." He took another pinch of snuff and sneezed violently.

"It is war, Monsieur Carruthers," he said bleakly. "War is a matter of life and death, is it not? Those who win, live; those who lose, die. Most unfortunate perhaps but there it is." He sneezed once again, explosively, like a small cannon. Then, with a wave of his hand I was dismissed without further argument. In short, I soon found myself alone in my dungeon once more, my freedom as far away as ever, though my lot was improved by the several "comforts" the Governor had seen fit to allow me.

Without my chains I was now free to walk about my gloomy cell, to pace out exactly the narrow boundaries of my domain. On a rough plank table now reposed a Bible, while beside it, throwing dark shadows, guttered a candle. I am ashamed to say that I gave no thanks for these mercies; instead I thought only about my misfortunes and nothing about the gifts that Heaven had given to me — not the least being my very life and the life of my friend. Despite my earlier ambitions regarding escape, that is, my hopes about Matthew and the help we might be, one to another, in this regard; despite, I say, all previous optimism, I was now so cast down in spirits that never in all my life was I so close to utter and complete despair.

For hours on end I tried tapping on the wall that separated our two cells, using the heel of my shoe, but alas, for all my monotonous effort I gained no answering response — and this failure, I think, was the main cause of my despair. Either the wall was too thick or the wretched jailer had told me a pointless lie and Turpin was in another part of the castle altogether. In the end I felt convinced that I was now quite alone, that only by my own efforts would I ever hope to escape. Looking about me, at the stone walls, the iron-bound door, and the barred window high above, I thought that, if ever I left this place it should be only in a coffin, that death alone would release me.

Sleep, when it came, gave me no comfort. As I lay on a

straw mattress in a corner, my dreams were full of those last dread moments when I saw Blunt. Always I saw the tortured face of The Bosun, saw him raise his arms, the wrists hung with chains. Once, before his specter faded into darkness, I fancied he pointed a skinny finger at me. I awoke, with a cry of terror, the moisture on my forehead, my hands clammy with fright.

In my extreme misery I at last sought refuge in my Bible, as indeed many a poor wretch has done before. As luck would have it the book fell open at Psalm twenty-three, the very words that Turpin had read aloud above the graves of the pirates, Smiley and Gimp. From this psalm I gained great comfort, nor did I feel so alone. How well I remember the change that soon took place in my feelings and how my heart felt lighter after the divine Word had fanned the dying embers of my courage! I well remember starting up and for some reason had the urge to turn out my pockets, as if taking stock of what humble blessings I might still have about me.

The first thing that I discovered was a hole in the lining of my pocket. Deep down among the cloth of my jacket I found, of all things, the present given to me by old Captain Campbell, he of the coasting brig *Caledonia*. After much fumbling I drew out the folding pocketknife. With a gasp of satisfaction I held it in my hand. There it was, all but forgotten, a good strong blade, also a steel point useful for picking stones from the hoofs of horses. Without a moment's hesitation I put the blade to good use by cutting a full inch from the bottom of my candle.

Well, I thought, if there's one treasure in the hole, how

many more? So I felt about below the lining to such good effect that I found a silver shilling, also a piece of flint. This last item was indeed a great discovery for I could now, with the aid of my steel knife and a little dry tinder, strike a light. So here was I on a sudden almost a man of wealth, where before I had nothing, not even my courage. Now I was determined to break out of my prison, come what may.

My candle was now extremely low. Almost a full hour had passed on this fateful evening, also I had cut short the candle's life by an inch at least, so that I reckoned only a scant five minutes remained to me of light before the jailer returned, as he always did, to remove the holder. Then I sat listening for the rattle of the door chains, hearing a vast downpour of rain from the outside. A loud clap of thunder echoed and reechoed about the towers and lightning flashed a brilliant blue through the small high window.

As I sat there, wishing most fervently that I might feel the rain on my face, I glimpsed a rat wandering about the dusty floor. Now you must know that rats were a common sight to me. Where they came from or how they moved from dungeon to dungeon had never, until now, caused me to ponder. Indeed I came to expect them, taking them for granted as a grim symbol of my captivity. But this particular rat was soaking wet. Water dripped from his bedraggled fur, his tail left a line of water in the dust. If rats I had often seen, a wet rat I had never seen before. Watching narrowly I tossed the horrid thing a small crust of bread. With a quick movement the rat seized it, and, running swiftly across the floor, vanished into a small hole at the very foot of the wall.

This hole I had never noticed before. My mind was now in a whirl of speculation. I placed my hand over the small opening at the base of the wall, where it met the floor. Immediately I felt a draft of air, faint but quite perceptible. Soaking wet from the rain, my friend — for a friend he surely was — had discovered a way in from the outside world. There was in fact, not one wall but two — and a hollow place between.

18

The Shaft and a Secret Door

It was now my task to chip away at the mortar around the stone where the hole was, my object being to remove this stone, thereby creating another door to my cell, a secret door leading to that hollow space between the walls so clearly revealed to me by the rat.

Now my knife was of such length that I could only at best remove half the mortar. The stone measured, at a guess, about eighteen inches square. By inserting my hand in the rat hole, I could feel the thickness of the wall　about a foot by my estimate. I also felt a strong updraft of air, like a chimney, so I was greatly encouraged in my efforts, being sure in my mind that somewhere beyond, either above or below, was another entry. Having thus a clear idea of what a vast amount of work lay before me, it was also clear that Captain Campbell's knife would be worn down long before the task was accomplished. I longed for a bar of iron at least a foot long, thin yet strong enough to crack the mortar. But where might such a splendid tool be found? Everywhere, except in a prison. The window was far too high — I even considered the bars — but though a fly might reach them I surely could not, even by standing precariously balanced on my table and stool.

Finally I examined the leg chains fastened to the wall by heavy iron spikes. If by chipping at the mortar around one of them — the weakest one I could find — if I should thereby wear out my knife, I might gain another sort of tool, a tool much handier for the important task. In short, I would exchange one tool for another and this I finally did, after a week of tedious work. In the end I pulled from the wall, like an old tooth, a spike of iron with the leg chain still attached. The chain made the tool clumsy to handle but I had no alternative other than to make the best of it.

Rusty and clumsy as it was, the iron was strong enough so that, by the end of three weeks' unremitting effort the stone came free. I had accomplished in that tedious length of time what any mason might have done in a morning, a simple statement that describes nothing of the agony experienced or the ever present danger of discovery that always threatened my endeavors.

I worked only after my jailer had left me early in the morning and after his last visit at night, though I was constantly on edge lest for some reason he might return, nor were my fears in this regard unfounded. One morning, after taking away my bowl and bucket, he suddenly returned. Fortunately, by listening to the church bells, I was able to estimate time very well and I always allowed a period to elapse before withdrawing my spike from its accustomed place in the wall. But I tell you I was about to lay my hands on it when I heard the rattle of chains at the door. Only a few seconds later and he would have discovered me, spike and all, scraping mortar from about the stone! He entered and took away my spoon which previously he had forgotten, also — good man — leaving me an extra crust of bread so that kindness as well as suspicion could be my undoing. After this fright, I waited a full hour though, as I say, I was always on edge, stopping and listening like a thief in a haunted house.

To hide all traces of my chipping I would stuff the empty space around the stone with straw mixed with mortar dust and dirt so that from a distance all seemed natural and undisturbed. As for the candle brought to me faithfully every evening, I never failed to remove a portion with the knife blade so that I managed to save up enough to last a good two hours. But these candle ends I put aside against the time I should need them later on, and learned to work tolerably well in the dark.

The mortar was old, and crumbled before the onslaught of the iron spike. My task became easier as the work progressed until the tool, being on the short side, could reach in no further. Then one night, shortly after twelve had sounded on the church bell, I gave the stone a hefty kick with my foot, almost sending it backwards down the shaft. To my relief, I managed to pull it back, drawing it completely out finally. So here at last was the prize I had so strenuously labored for: a hole in the wall big enough for me to stick my head and shoulders through.

Trembling from excitement, I somehow managed, with

the aid of my flint, to light one of the candle ends. Impatience did not make the task easier, I can tell you, but after much fretting and blowing on tinder I was presently able to shine a little light through the hole.

The opposite wall was no more than three feet away, so close that I put my hand out and touched it. The surface was exceedingly rough, with jagged ends of stone and deep crevices offering almost as good a foothold as a ladder. Beyond the modest circle of light thrown by the candle, I could see little. Downward or upward was a deep blackness, but all the while the flame in my hand wivered and wavered in the steady cold draft of air from below. This, then, was all I saw that night.

I slept deeply, like a dead man, so utterly tired that I awakened only when the jailer rattled the door chains outside. He looked around suspiciously — or so my conscience said — and I was in a state of terror lest he discover my secret. But the stone was in place, the mortar cracks filled in most convincingly, and the iron spike likewise returned to its original hole, so that nothing could betray me except he make a close inspection. As it was, he went about his business and left me. Not a word passed between us.

My activities now became exceedingly dangerous. If he returned when I was absent from my cell all would, of course, be lost — unless I had made good my final escape. This was a great risk but there was no way of getting around it. I made a fair dummy figure with my jacket, boots, and straw from the mattress so that if he merely glanced through the panel he might think I slept and be satisfied. Thus I prepared the way, as best I could, for the first exit from my dungeon.

Waiting, with great impatience, until the noon bell had struck, I finally eased the stone back and peered down the shaft.

To my great joy I saw daylight — a brilliant sunbeam — coming from a small opening, not more than twenty feet down. This light was so reflected that I could easily make out all the crevices and rough juttings of stone in the wall. In a moment I crawled through my hatch and was inside the shaft.

My feet were bare, all the better to feel for every crevice; my fingers clung to every outcrop and so I worked my way downward, like a mountain climber. Ties of stone there were, from wall to wall, put there by the masons, and these stone rungs were of great assistance; in short, to climb down was hardly more difficult than climbing down a ladder, while to climb upward (as I discovered) was no more difficult than climbing the mast of a ship.

Once arrived at the bottom I found the ground a mass of broken masonry and stones. Curiosity drove me to explore but I found nothing remarkable there. I think that, at one time, it had been a shaft for drawing up water to the various floors of the castle, from a well now long since filled in. Indeed I discovered an old pulley and a bucket, also a circular depression still faintly visible. But of useful bars of iron I found nothing, so I was left with my old leg-chain spike, or what remained of it.

The small hole to the outside world was nothing more than an opening for a drain tile, being less than half a foot in diameter. Flat on my stomach, ignoring the horrible roughness of the stones, I looked through, seeing a narrow ledge of rock with a few weeds growing between the cracks. Beyond was sea and sky, a sea so green and a sky so blue that words cannot describe my feelings when I gazed on this wondrous scene for the first time.

The chain, with the attached spike, I had carried looped about my waist. Using a stone for a hammer, I now attacked the drain hole. The work was painfully slow. By the time the church bells tolled three o'clock I had made the hole big enough to allow passage of my head.

I debated whether to go back to my dungeon, the risk being awful that my absence would be discovered. But I am by nature foolhardy and the closer I came to freedom, the more reckless I became. Working with a frenzy of energy (having decided to stay only another half hour) I quite forgot the passing of time. First four, then five struck. Presently I stopped, the hole still not wide enough. I wiped the sweat from my brow with my shirt sleeve, listening to the chimes of the village bell, counting each peal. To my dismay I counted six. Six o'clock! At any moment my jailer would be about his rounds for the evening!

Like a mountain goat I leaped up the wall, my heart racing with anxiety. No mainmast was ever climbed so speedily. Reaching the opening to my cell I crawled through, pushed the stone shut and, with trembling fingers managed to stuff the imitation mortar into the cracks. I then dismantled the dummy figure and donned my jacket and shoes — all this accomplished in as much time as it takes to tell of it. Then, to my horror, I found that my iron spike, the spike that must always be in its accustomed place in the wall, was missing, left behind at the foot of the shaft!

The hole, to my terrified eyes, seemed to gape like a cave. There was nothing for it except to place the old plank table in such a position in front of it that my jailer would, I hoped, fail to notice it. I sat down on my little three-legged stool, opened my Bible and began, with fear in my heart, to read as best I could by the dim light. Hardly had I done so than the sliding panel opened, the door chains rattled and my jailer was inside with my evening meal of bread and meat.

"You sleep this afternoon, yes?" said he.

"Oh yes," said I, gulping with panic.

"Blind you will be, reading in such a light. The candle I bring. Then you read."

"Very well," said I, in a whisper. "Thank you very much."

"You have the illness?" said he. "Pale you look. You inside too much, eh?" He grinned at his own joke. I smiled weakly. Then he was gone. Almost at once he returned, set a lighted candle on the table in front of me and left again. This time, as I knew, he would not return for an hour or more and I lost no time in retrieving the spike with the attached leg chain from the bottom of the shaft.

Well, this was a great fright to me and I determined to finish the escape hole that very night. Thus it came about that one o'clock in the morning found me descending the shaft with a candle stub. Before the birds began to chirp I had enlarged the hole enough so that a man could crawl through. My path to freedom was now complete and it only remained for me to somehow conjure Matthew Turpin into my dungeon so that together we might escape.

19

A Plan of Escape

NEXT MORNING I asked the jailer if I might speak with my friend, if only for a minute or two. He shook his head.

"The Governor give strict orders," said he. "If I let you have talk together they will flog me. You must not ask me to do this." His eyes were full of suspicion. For a moment I was sorry that I had mentioned the matter. Hoping to make things easier, I then presented him with my shilling, saying that I had given up all hope of leaving the prison, that I only wanted to give my friend a message for my family if he should, by some chance, be released. This explanation, plus the shilling, seemed to satisfy the jailer. He bit the coin, looked at it curiously, then, with a shrug, put it in his pocket.

"No chance your friend be set free," he said. "He already try once to escape. Not try again I think for a long time."

I quailed inwardly at this ominous news. He sensed my concern, I think, and to do him credit, took pains to relieve my mind.

"Very brave man, your friend," said he. "When I took him to see the Governor, Monsieur Picard, he suddenly break away, run into courtyard where soldiers are. He leap on horse, al-

163

most reach gate, too. Very good on horse, your friend. Very brave man."

Also very reckless, I thought grimly. He then told me how Turpin had been stopped at the main gate leading to the town. Without a weapon, he had, nevertheless, fought furiously with the guards and in the melee had been shot in the arm, though, as the jailer reassured me, not seriously.

"Do not worry, boy," he said. "Your friend all recovered now. But he I watch like a hawk. No escape for him, never fear that."

After the jailer had gone I pondered and thought and racked my brains how to get Turpin into my cell and somehow arrange matters that we be left alone to effect our escape. The problem drove me almost to despair. There seemed to be only one way: to spend endless strength and days dislodging yet another stone, either from the wall that separated my cell from the next, or a stone from inside the shaft opposite his cell — and this terrible amount of work could be all for nothing if he was lodged elsewhere in the fortress. Each time I had mentioned his whereabouts the jailer only shook his head and I think the man was under strict orders not to tell me. Also, my only tool, the leg chain spike, was now pitifully worn down.

Then I remembered the jailer remarking on my health — "You have the illness? Pale, you look" — without a doubt I suddenly felt quite pale and sickly, also exceedingly hungry for a slice of roast or a good mutton pie, so that the thought of food alone made me feel weak as a kitten. The more I thus considered my symptoms, the more unwell I felt. It is a fair marvel how a person can think himself into a state of collapse. By the time my jailer came with the evening ration, I was lying prone on my mattress, groaning and tossing like a man in the last throes of a terrible fever.

"You ill?" he asked, frowning, bending over me so that I could smell the wine on his breath. "Prison fever you have, or possibly the plague."

"No," I gasped, "not that; I mean, it isn't the plague. It's a kind of pain I have, in my stomach; also a pain in my head."

All this was certainly true enough, for my stomach was painfully empty; as for my head, it was racked with anxiety. At the mention of the word *plague,* he backed hurriedly away, crossing himself and muttering. I groaned and moaned, begging him in piteous tones to fetch Monsieur Picard.

"Remember, I gave you a shilling," I whispered. "This may be a last favor I ask of you."

The jailer hurried away, leaving a bowl of watery soup with a few pieces of gray meat floating in it. I longed to gulp the mess down (the very sight of the bowl almost drove me mad) but persons near death's door are not likely to have much of an appetite so I controlled myself and the jailer returned presently with alarming news.

"The Governor he is at table now," he said, rolling his eyes. "Ah, Monsieur, the fine wine, the giant roast, the valuable silver — you should see it!"

I gnashed my teeth. My stomach felt empty as a drum. The jailer loomed over me as I lay gasping on my pallet of straw. He seemed immensely pleased about something and

165

stood there, arms folded, a heavy ring of keys hanging from a belt about his middle.

"A rumor I have heard that he will take you from this dungeon," he said. "A more comfortable place, high up in the east tower. You will like it there, Monsieur." The idiot nodded and smiled. "Oh yes, you will be much pleased, I am sure. Lucky you are, eh?"

I groaned and turned my face to the wall. The possibility of being moved had never occurred to me. I thought of the endless hours I had spent — bitter, toiling hours, every one — chipping and hacking at stone, all to gain my freedom, all gone to nought, all for nothing. Thinking of it made me ill in truth; I had no need to pretend. I felt ill enough to give up the ghost from bitter disappointment.

He went briskly out about his business. Once more I was alone. In my great anxiety I managed to polish off the little supper he had left. What could it matter now, I thought, since all my hopes for freedom were lost; I might as well ease my hunger.

I had a notion to escape alone, then and there, but conscience makes cowards of us all. I struggled with the pros and cons of leaving Matthew, as it were, in the lurch, but before I could make up my mind one way or the other, the Governor himself arrived at my door, accompanied by the jailer, also a holy man dressed all in black and wearing a hat shaped like a boat.

"What is this?" cried General Picard striding in. "Our young prisoner is not well? Prison life does not agree with you, Monsieur Carruthers? But that is what prisons are for

— to make you sorry for your sins, is it not so?" He too bent over me, clucking his tongue, talking rapidly in French to the holy man, who likewise examined me, pulling down my eyelid and poking me so that I felt like a joint of meat in a butcher's shop. The jailer, I could see through half-closed eyes, hung back, no doubt afraid he might catch the dreaded plague.

Meanwhile I did my part (since there seemed nothing else to do) by groaning and putting hand to forehead like a young girl ready to faint. The Governor looked about as if he had never set foot in a dungeon before — as I daresay he hadn't.

"Bah! This damp cellar, it is no place for a boy. Immediately you must be removed. To a new dry clean dungeon you must go — now, this minute!"

I groaned in desperation, the holy man nodded and spoke a few words of agreement in his own tongue. I groaned again; the holy man made the sign of the cross.

"No, if you please, sir," said I in a faint voice. "My last hour has come, I fear. To move me now must only hasten my end. Perhaps tomorrow, if I should live."

"Well, we shall see," said Picard. "Meanwhile, if there is anything we can do, Monsieur Carruthers."

"I have only one request to make," said I. "One last favor." My voice sank to a whisper.

"Mon Dieu! name it, boy. We French are not fiends."

"Then I beg of you, sir," said I, "let me speak a last word with my old friend, Mr. Turpin."

At that he gave a start of surprise. I could see the quick anger in his face. The holy man took off his hat and fanned me with it. I thought him very kind.

"Turpin! A scoundrel, that fellow is," he cried, waving his hands. "My soldiers he attack; a horse he try to steal. He is not only a scoundrel, he is mad!"

Secretly I agreed, most fervently. The holy man looked grave and nodded his head.

"He is my countryman," said I, coughing piteously. "We have faced many dangers together and he has saved my life more than once. It is only natural that I should want to speak to him before I leave this world."

"A passing indisposition, Monsieur," said Picard, with a frown. "We have many young fellows like you, Monsieur Carruthers, fighting for Napoleon. Every day they suffer but do not complain."

"Then you refuse my request?" said I, turning my face to the wall. "You refuse to let me speak with my friend for the last time?" I groaned and coughed again.

A thought struck me, a sudden inspiration. I remembered the diamonds. It was the holy man, I think, who brought them to mind. He was fingering his beads in the manner typical of his religion. Click, click, they went and in a flash I remembered the fabulous necklace.

Struggling up on one elbow, I then told Picard (interrupted by much coughing and groaning) that I had knowledge, secret knowledge, that would save Turpin's life. In short, I hinted to the Governor that I knew the whereabouts of a certain diamond necklace, a royal necklace of great value. Never did I see a man change his expression so quickly or so completely. His eyes narrowed, all the former joviality of

manner drained away. A mask, it seemed, had quite dropped and beneath it all he appeared as greedy and ruthless as a wolf at the kill. To my astonishment he pulled, from a pocket in his fine velvet jacket, a pistol and held it to my head.

"Now, Monsieur Carruthers," he said grimly, "I think you understand more than you tell, eh? This necklace you speak of: did it once belong to France?"

"As to that, sir," I whispered (not forgetting for a moment how very ill I was), "as to that I do not know. It once belonged to Mr. Blunt, I'm quite sure it did."

He grunted. The rim of his pistol was cold against my

temple. I shivered and the holy man clucked his tongue in shocked disapproval at the scene.

"And did you take it from Monsieur Blunt?" asked Picard.

"It may well be that I did," said I. "Then again perhaps not."

"Boy, unless you reveal all you know," said he, trembling with rage, "I shall shoot you through the head like a dog."

"You may as well," said I faintly, turning up my eyes. "What do I care now if you kill me? I suffer great pain. My end is very close, I can feel it. Kill me, by all means, sir, and may God forgive you. If I die before speaking to my friend, no one will ever find the necklace. The secret will die with me." I sank back and closed my eyes.

He gave a gasp of exasperation. Then the pistol, as I could see through eyes not quite closed, slowly retreated back into his jacket pocket. The holy man uttered a few low soothing words and once again fanned me with his hat.

"This man Turpin — why do you wish to tell him about this matter?" said Picard.

Uttering a weary sigh I looked at him standing over me, his face red with anger.

"Because, sir, my friend has been unjustly accused of stealing. If I can but help him before I die, to help right this wrong, why, sir, I shall die a happier man than I am now."

Picard turned away. The holy man spoke to him in low tones, though what passed between them I had no way of knowing. Then the Governor spoke sharply to the jailer, who immediately, with a bow, left the cell.

"Very well, boy," said Picard, his face very set and angry,

"your request I shall grant. Ten minutes alone with this fellow you shall have. I would not allow it, ordinarily. But there is more to these matters than the eye sees. Within the hour, I shall have a little talk with Monsieur Turpin — and we have special methods of dealing with people who steal the treasures of France!"

Then, with a last baleful look at me, he left, followed by the good man dressed in black.

Shortly after, as I lay sweating, my heart pounding with anxiety, the jailer and two soldiers brought in Matthew Turpin. He looked haggard, his cheeks were very sunken and his arm was bandaged with a dirty rag. The guards swung shut the iron-bound door.

I listened until the last rattle of the lock chains had died away. Then, with only a bare word of greeting to Matthew, I leaped up and started to pull away the stone from the wall.

20

Escape at Last

"Dear boy, what in the devil's name are you up to?" gasped Matthew, astonished by my fumbling at the stone and then stunned by finding it come away to reveal the hole. Feet first I entered, edging downward on the little shelves of rock, feeling, with trembling hands, for the familiar crevices and irregularities of the wall.

"Do as I do," I said curtly. "In you come. Pull the stone shut if you can — it might gain us a minute if they not find the opening."

I heard him gasping and struggling as his legs came over the side and with terror in my heart heard him slip. A small shower of dust and small bits of masonry almost blinded me but I managed to look down in time.

"If you fall, you fall on me; we'll both go crashing down, so mind," said I. "Hang on. It isn't too hard if you're careful. Feel for a stone first with your hands, then feel for another with your feet. It's like a ladder, you'll see."

"Like a ladder, is it?" he gasped, beginning to move down. "I hope it's not far, that's all. I'm not a bloomin' monkey, you know. Ladder, you call it! Some ladder! I'll break my neck before I'm done."

"Come on," I said urgently. "They'll be back in no time."

By now I was halfway down and could see a faint blur of daylight below. Dusk had fallen; in another half hour darkness would be to our advantage. For a man who never climbed higher than was necessary to reach a saddle, Matthew did well enough, though he fell the last few feet and barked his shins. I was already crawling through to the outside world when I heard the crash, followed by a yell and a deal of cursing and swearing.

I hissed back at him, "You're a fine one to make all that noise; there's no time to waste on a few scratches." Then I helped him through the hole and he was glad enough to breathe the outside air.

"A fair marvel, you are, Steve," he said, balancing himself pretty gingerly on the narrow ledge. A few stones rattled down the cliff face and I prayed there were no guards to glance up and see us.

"A fair marvel, that's all I can say," he gasped, wiping a dirty sleeve over his face. "How you did it I don't know. I'd rather face an army alone than go through that again."

"You'll fall into the sea if you don't watch," I said sharply. "This perch isn't more than a yard wide."

He groaned and shut his eyes.

"How far down is it?" he asked.

I glanced over. "Not more than two hundred feet. Come on, the ledge slopes down. We'd best crawl along."

He muttered, "Two hundred feet! I'll never hold up another coach as long as I live, I swear!"

And I'll never take one, I thought. If I can't find a ship — any ship — why then I'll walk and be all the safer for it.

A hundred feet of sheer cliff still lay beneath us when the ledge came to a sudden end. Putting my arm out before me, I felt only emptiness.

"What's the bad news now?" he whispered at my heels.

"Oh it's not so bad if you've got wings," I said, "but we either stay here, go back, or make a jump for it. "There's a gap."

"Well then, a tree grows just above," said he. "If you can sight the other side, I've a mind to swing across."

Sure enough, an old stubborn pine, common on that part of the coast, had rooted in the cliff face. Little more than a bush it was, all twisted by sea and wind. Looking across I thought the ledge continued, only wider. The distance between was perhaps ten feet, a chancy guess in that light. But I could only give him my opinion and small encouragement since we had a choice of breaking our necks then and there or dying by inches in a French prison — unless they shot us down like pigeons, which seemed very likely.

He said he would try it first and if he got across I surely could. So I huddled against the cliff face while he first tested the tree; then, being satisfied on that score, managed to climb out on the furthest limb. I looked up, my head swimming at the risk he took, but he managed it, dropping down on the opposite ledge with a low shout of triumph. In the dark I could barely see a pale glimmer from his shirt but it served as a mark. Up I went into the tree and swung across without mishap, finding our footing much improved since the path was now a good deal wider.

But hardly was this obstacle overcome when a loud clamor of bells rang out from the town above. Every church it seemed was in league to warn the populace of our escape. Picard had discovered our flight and the hunt was on.

We had, by this time, come much closer to the strand. The whispering of the waves had grown to a steady never-ending thunder. It was possible now to run down the widening path and in a flurry of sand we at last reached the end of the path and the beginning of a wide beach. Here we paused, the clang of bells all about us, looking fearfully up and down, seeing by the light of the rising moon a cluster of dockside buildings, also a pier jutting out into the sea. On our right, if we continued on, were stone steps leading upward from the beach to a narrow street of the town. It was up this very street we had marched on our way to Saint-Malo prison.

"Stop for a minute," I said, catching my breath. "A plan we must have, some agreement, or we only wander about like lost sheep." I flung myself down, panting and weary, in the shadow of the steps.

"The question is, dear boy," said Matthew, sitting beside me, "do we lose ourselves in town among the population or keep walking along the beach?"

"And what do you say?" said I, having already made up my mind.

"If you seek to outwit the enemy, then you must always do what he least expects," said he, flinging a stone toward the water. "Now for me, going to town and finding us two

good horses — why lad, on horseback we can likely reach
Spain in a week or even Holland, if you prefer."

"What the enemy may expect is one thing," said I, grimly.
"What I intend doing is another. Spain is a bonny place, no
doubt, and there's good cheese in Holland. Enjoy it, for all I
care. I hope you find a horse. But as for me, I'm off to find a
fishing boat. I can tell you, I know where I'm going — and
it's neither of those places."

I got up and started off toward the edge of the sea where
the tide came swirling in. The waves licked my shoes, shoes
now sadly in need of mending. The bells, to my relief, suddenly ceased ringing, and when I glanced up toward the
road I saw people beginning to congregate while lamps and
one or two flares could be seen. Our place of capture, the
stores shed, I recognized very well, outlined by the light of
the moon. If the little boat still rode at anchor there, why
then I had a notion to take it and sail away, regardless of the
consequences. I might be sunk by cannon or wrecked by a
storm — so be it, I thought, for I would rather die beneath
the cold green sea than slowly rot away among the rats.

Sure enough the boat was there, the dockside silent and
deserted. I passed the shed, keeping a wary eye for pickets
but saw nothing that moved except an old cat running close
against the wall.

But footsteps I heard and it was Matthew running up,
bold as you please, without a thought we might once again
meet trouble in the same place.

"Steve, I have no liking to tour Spain," he said, in a low

voice. "If you've no objection, I'd just as soon help with the boat."

"Very well," I said, rather pleased than not, "but you'll do as I say, remember. There's not room for two captains on a ship."

"Every man to his own trade," said he, in a humble tone, new to him. "I have no false pride on that score. If you'll bear with me, though, I've just remembered the pistols. A fair shame it would be to leave 'em for Napoleon."

Before I could say yes or no, he had run off into the shed, leaving me to deal with the mooring lines.

By this time a murmur of noise, coming from a crowd of people, drew closer and closer. Without a doubt it was soldiers looking for us. Then suddenly one of them, a little ahead of the rest, saw me and shouted something in French. Not receiving an answer, he leveled his musket and fired. This, of course, was a signal to the rest and they came charging toward me, all yelling and firing off weapons. Behind them I glimpsed a mob of people flourishing pitchforks, scythes and knives affixed to poles.

A gang of men were now close to the steps leading down to the beach, some holding flaming torches. A bullet whistled by my head as Matthew came running out of the shed carrying a sack of meal. As he jumped nimbly into the boat I cast off the stern line. Then, grabbing the oars, I maneuvered her out past the head of the dock into open water, just as the crowd came pouring onto the beach.

A fast pinnace shot out from the far side of the dock with

four soldiers rowing. I gave it two minutes before they caught us.

"Have you the pistols?" I yelled at Matthew huddled in the stern.

"Yes, each one loaded," he sang out. "But no extra powder or ball. I'll wait until they come closer."

Thus we had two shots only; also there was a fair swell and this would make his aim the more uncertain.

The pinnace came up quickly, I could hear the men yelling as they rowed. Then a musket was fired and the ball sang past my head, followed a moment later by the crack of Matthew's pistol. There was a loud cry, then I saw one of them fall into the sea. They had to stop and waste a good deal of time pulling him out and this caused such a delay that we

drew away rapidly. Also our actions must now convince them of our true colors: in other words there was no chance of our escaping alive from this fight if we should lose it.

On they came. A man suddenly stopped rowing — I could see him quite clearly outlined against the moon — and he pointed a musket, rising a little from his seat. Before he could pull the trigger, Matthew fired off his last pistol and the soldier toppled sideways into the sea, musket and all. Everyone to his own trade, I thought.

Then, without warning, a great explosion came from the quartermaster's stores and a tongue of flame burst through the roof. The sea around was now a mirror of red glare, even the sky rained down fire as pieces of burning wood fell, with a hiss, into the water. The shed was, in the space of a moment, a roaring, crackling inferno. Mouth open, I gazed at this fearful sight, thinking how my friend Turpin had done more than retrieve his pistols from the French.

I had no mind to ask questions at that time, however, and he said nothing, only looked unsmiling and grim. When I told him to pull on the halyard and raise sail, he leaped to it so that we quickly drew away from the coast before a good strong breeze.

The last I saw of France was a somber headland with the moon behind it, and a red glare. I watched and watched, my hand on the tiller, thinking how we came there with flame — and left the same way. War is a time of dark journeys, I thought, and the way is often lit with fire.

The light gradually dimmed. After a while all that remained was darkness and the heaving, roaring sea.

21

A Mystery Is Solved

U<small>NTIL</small> WE had a safe distance between us and the French coast, I ordered Matthew to rest while I kept watch and worked the vessel. A strict watch was necessary since we had no certainty of being safe: we might either be pursued or meet a patrol ship, all this quite apart from the normal perils of the sea and wind. So, as I say, I told him to sleep until such time as I thought we had got clean away, though he protested, demanding the first watch, but I had my will in the matter.

Our vessel was small, being not above sixteen feet, and I think she must have served as a tender or a ferry of some kind. She had one mast with a leg-of-mutton sail, a queer tubby sort of craft, comical to look at. She bobbed up and down like a cork. I half expected Matthew to be ill but he curled up in the bow without further complaint, covering himself with an old canvas and that was the last I heard of him.

A little compass was screwed down near the tiller but since the oil lamp was dry, I could see nothing of the needle in the pitch dark. The moon had long since vanished, but I found north by the polestar, my one objective being to clear the coast as quickly as possible.

An old woolen shirt that I presently found in a locker was a great relief from the cold. Putting the thing on, I found myself stinking horribly of fish but smell or not, it served its purpose, though my teeth chattered, despite all my efforts to control them, for a long time.

How desperately I longed for food! If only the sea were a lamb stew or even hot porridge, why I would think we sailed in Heaven! After a time my mind began to wander. I became dazed and thought I heard voices, but when I cried out in answer, there was nothing except the eerie sound of the wind and hissing waves.

Matthew sat up presently (I believe my mad shouting awakened him) and he took the tiller from my numb hands. After that I have no clear recollection of events beyond falling instantly into a black pit of dreamless sleep.

When I awoke I found the world much changed: the sun just up, and the waves gleaming gold in the east.

"Good morning, dear boy," said Matthew cheerfully. "Breakfast, you will be glad to hear, is now being served."

Then, to my joy, he presented me with a tin mug of hot salty porridge — the very stuff, as it were, of my delirium! The oats he had stolen from the stores shed; as for the cooking of it, he had found a square rusty tin box somewhere in the boat and made from it a miniature stove. The thing was most cleverly contrived, though how he managed to fire the awful damp fuel — old rope, bits of wood and such like odds and ends, I shall never know. But if he was in many ways unscrupulous and reckless, he was also clever and resourceful. Indeed I have learned on many desperate occasions that cleverness is not confined to those who are scrupulous or steady in their habits, nor, for that matter, is a brave heart always pure.

As you can imagine, I ate the porridge with great relish and enjoyed more than one helping, not caring much if it was entirely cooked or not. So, all in all, our hunger was relieved, but not our thirst for there was not a drop of fresh water in the boat.

About noon by the sun we sighted, on the western horizon, a brig. The breeze was more in our favor so by the time she lay dead ahead she was also close enough to recognize. There was no doubt in my mind that she was English.

She turned toward us and, when close enough, fired off a cannon. The ball fell with a great splash not ten feet short of our bowsprit.

"This is too much," grumbled Turpin bitterly. "First we're thrown into prison by the French, now we're fired on by the English! I'm going to fight for the Turks, see if I don't!"

Glancing up at our masthead, I immediately pulled off my shirt.

"You can't blame the captain," I said, laughing. "If we fly French colors why then we must look out for trouble."

I hauled down the tattered pennant that, all unknown to us, had fluttered at our peak; then I bent on my shirt to take its place and very odd it looked as a flag, though it served its new purpose well enough for there was no more firing at us from the brig.

She hove to, looking tall and grand as we came close. Her name I made out on the bow and she was *The Alerte* of Bristol. Never was I more glad to see a ship. I looked up at her steep sides, saw the row of seamen's faces looking down, and I can tell you there was such a lump in my throat that I could hardly speak.

"Ye've a queer taste in flags," yelled the Captain, through a speaking trumpet. "Are ye in distress?"

"Oh yes, sir," said I. "We need food and water, also our position, if you'd be kind enough."

"Where are ye bound in that washtub?" said he.

"Plymouth," said I.

"Well, well. I'll take ye myself," said he. "I'm short-handed. Can ye work yer passage?"

"Oh yes, sir," said I eagerly. "If you know Captain Campbell of the *Caledonia* he'll surely give me a reference."

There was a moment's silence. Then he shouted at me again, through the trumpet.

"If ye pass muster with old Campbell, ye'll do fine for me, boy! Is yer friend handy on a ship?"

"No sir," said I. "He's more for the cavalry. But he's a rare shot with a pistol, and that's handy enough and useful if we meet pirates."

"Aye, well, since you're a friend of Campbell's," said he, "I'll make his passage half price — two guineas instead of four. I'll have a tackle sent down for the both of ye."

The sea was calm, with only a gentle swell, so I had no difficulty in keeping, with the aid of an oar, our little craft clear of the brig's side. Matthew sat beside me on the middle thwart.

"I'm not going, Steve," said he, quickly. "I've important business ashore, near Moorefields, so I'll sail on, if it's all the same to you."

I was utterly dumfounded.

"Sail on?" I repeated, letting the oar drop. "What ever can you mean? With the brig we'll be in port in no time. It's a sight more comfortable, and there's something in the way of food. You must be mad."

"Aye, the brig's tempting, I must admit," said he, with a sigh. "But I may as well tell you now and get it over. You see, I hid the diamonds in the attic of the old mill. I've a mind to recover them and make my fortune."

"Then you lied all the time," said I. "You said often and enough that you never had the diamonds. You told Blunt so, in front of me."

"Nor did I have 'em — they were hid, as I say, in the attic, safe and sound," said he.

"And where pray did you come by them?" said I, astonished at all this.

"Well, it was Smiley. He took the necklace from Blunt's box, after the coach turned over. Before I buried Smiley and Gimp I turned out their pockets, if you remember, and gave Sweeney any money I found. It was then I found the diamonds — on Smiley. Then I hid 'em in the mill. I had no intention of giving 'em up to Jenkyns and his lot. Do you blame me?"

He looked very unhappy and crestfallen. Our boat nudged gently against the brig. I pushed her off a bit with the oar.

"If you tell me where you'll be, Steve," said he earnestly, " — if you give me a lawyer's name or a bank, why lad, I'll share with you equals. I've no mind to hog it all for myself. It was your doing, our escape from the prison. You've fair earned your share."

"It's all yours, Matthew Turpin," I said. "Not one farthing would I touch — ever. I hope you do well by the money."

"But why, dear boy?" he pleaded. "It's a fortune — and all yours, for nothing. You'll not see the like of it again, I'll be bound."

"There isn't anything in this world for nothing," said I. "You'll pay for the diamonds in the end, like all the rest did — Deadlock, Smiley, Gimp, Sweeney and Mr. Blunt — all of 'em. Where are they now, I ask you? As for me, it's all been a fine experience, and that's payment enough."

The rope came down from the masthead pulley.

"Are ye all ready below?" yelled the Captain. "I'm late now, so shake a leg!"

I grasped the rope firmly and placed my foot in the sling of the tackle. The crew heaved on the line and I began to rise in the air, slowly turning.

"One last thing," I said. "You'll find my box in the cottage. You took it from me, remember, when I went to Moorefields that night."

"Let me know where to send it, Steve," he cried, looking very unhappy.

"All I want from it is my late uncle's telescope," said I. "Send it to me, care of Captain Mullins at the Admiralty. Good-by, Matthew — and good luck!"

"Good-by, Stevie," he said, looking up. There was a sad note in his voice. Then he lifted his hand in farewell, a solemn gesture that was almost a benediction. As I stepped over the side of *The Alerte* he pushed off with the oar and was soon falling away behind our stern, the little sail fully out to a good breeze.

And that was the last I ever saw of Matthew Turpin.

We reached Plymouth finally after a slow, uneventful voyage. I immediately sought out Captain Mullins at the Jollyboat Inn and was pleasantly surprised to find him there.

"You must excuse me for being tardy," said he, shaking my hand. "We left a month late and had bad weather all the way."

"Well, sir, I'm rather late myself," said I, sitting down at his supper table in the inn parlor, "and it wasn't entirely the fault of the weather."

He lifted his mug of ale and wished me health.

"Did you run into trouble?" said he.

"Yes, in a manner of speaking," said I, cutting up my beef.

"Tell me all about it," said he.

And I did.